The Angel Doll

The Angel Doll

Margaret Joanne Rice

The Angel Doll

J. Kenkade Publishing
6104 Forbing Rd
Little Rock, AR 72209
www.jkenkadepublishing.com
Facebook.com/jkenkadepublishing

J. Kenkade Publishing is a registered trademark.

Printed in the United States of America
ISBN 978-1-944486-87-7

Contents

Chapter 1

The Warning and the Flight to Bellingfast

"Did you have a nice visit with Aunt Glenora?"

"Yes, Mother, it was very nice." Constance shared with her mother her reluctance to return to Bellingfast.

"Oh, darling Constance," tutted her mother. "You erase that terrible experience from your mind. It has almost been three years, and now it is time to get on with your life. Lady Lindsey and I both agree that the angel doll is just foolishness and an old Negro wives' tale. Mac will meet us at Parkview Plantation later this afternoon."

"Will you all be leaving soon? "Constance asked.

"Yes, probably by the end of the week. We will be returning to Paris to finish the business transactions. Hopefully, the auction will begin next month." Her mother paused and then said, "But Constance, I am concerned about you. I know you are very scared about returning to Ireland."

"Yes, Mother, I am very scared. However, Lady Lindsey has assured me that we will be safe. She will be my traveling companion, and I will feel a lot safer with her traveling with me."

"Yes, Constance, she is a darling of a sister. I don't know what I would have done over the years if I had not had her help."

"But, Mama, I do miss you a lot. I always remember the summer we spent on Carolina Beach and the mountain climbing adventures in Colorado. It was so much fun when I was little, and you were not so busy with your business. I even enjoyed being with you in Paris when you would do your winter shopping.

"However, I remember that terrible finishing school in Holland. It was so dull. All I remember is counting the months off the calendar, just waiting until I could return to Parkview Plantation to be with Lady Lindsey, Aunt Glenora, and Virginia Camille, when she spent the summers with us. The girls from the finishing school were so snooty, and I never seemed to fit in with them."

"Oh, darling, I do remember that. You did have a hard time at school," her mother said thoughtfully. "And, darling, that is precisely why we encouraged you to take up writing. Your writing has been a blessing and a lifesaver."

"It has," Constance agrees. "I must admit that when I write, I can take my mind to a whole new world."

"I do hope you finish your novel."

"And, Mama, I know you want me to find a nice, cultured gentleman, fall in love, and get married."

"Yes, darling Constance, that would be grand. Lady Lindsey tells us that the richest and most eligible bachelors from around the globe schedule years in advance to attend Madam MaRooska's fantastic events. Many young men have been on her list for years before they were accepted. The most intriguing, exciting, and influential people from around the world want to experience this spectacular event at her parties.

"This is all quite understandable; the young men want to be able to meet the finest young ladies from around the globe. Madam MaRooska's strategy games are known worldwide. They are full of adventure, danger, and excitement. As a matter of fact, Constance, I do kind of envy you, dear. The experiences do sound remarkable."

Constance Stallings was a bright young lady who had been shuffled around all her life while her mother was traveling. Her mother was Eunice Clarice Stallings. Eunice's second husband traveled the world over trying to increase their fortunes. Clarice was a bit spoiled, and when Constance was born, Clarice was not ready for motherhood. Lady Lindsey, Clarice's older sister, had never married and enjoyed watching after her niece. In fairness, Lady Lindsey had raised Constance. Glenora Rushing was another elderly aunt; she had lived most of her years at Parkview Plantation. For the past ten years, Glenora had been in a wheelchair and was in a nursing home. When Constance was home for the summer, she would spend hours at the nursing home visiting Aunt Glenora. The two would spend hours talking and laughing. Aunt Glenora had taught Constance to knit and crochet. When Constance decided to become a writer, Aunt Glenora introduced her to several of her personal friends who were authors. Through their acquaintance, Constance developed a strong desire to study literature, especially pertaining to old southern customs and legends of the Negro slaves in Southern Louisiana.

In North Myrtle Beach, South Carolina, there sat a large beach house on the water where Constance's family lived.

The phone rang, and the housemaid answered. "No ma'am, the Admiral is not in. He will not be in until Thursday. May I ask who is calling?"

There were a few pauses between her answers. "Yes… no…yes…Miss Stallings isn't in. She and a school chum are out shopping in Georgetown. Would you like her to return your call? Okay, thanks, and congratulations to you. To reach your eightieth birthday is quite remarkable. I will have Miss Camille return your call. She will be in later this afternoon. She will be pleased that you called. She is looking forward to going to Bellingfast for Madam MaRooska's event."

The hustle and bustle of shopping never changed. Virginia Camille thought she was buying the store out. Last year's style would never do. For an aristocratic southern debutante with class and culture, Virginia Camille enjoyed playing the part. She played it with much dignity. Her long, sun-bleached hair flowed in the wind. Her slim body frame adhered to the ocean front, as she spent the largest percentage of her life at her father's yacht club. The Admiral had done quite well for himself. Navy life was good for him, but when he retired, he headed back to Myrtle Beach's North Shore. He had grown up there as a child. He developed a love for the water and a love for challenging investments. Having invested his assets wisely, he and Virginia Camille had lived quite comfortably for their entire life together. He was a very distinguished elderly man, who was graying around his temples. He had had many lady acquaintances from around the globe, including royals and celebrities. Many of the women had wished for a more permanent relationship, but the Admiral had no plans for a marriage commitment of this sort. He had traveled the world and was extremely active in international affairs.

The limo was parked outside Parkview Plantation. When Clarice and Constance approached the door, the housemaid opened it.

"You all are late," the housemaid remarked. "Dinner is on the table. Wash up and join the group in the dining hall."

"Thank you, Ardenia," Clarice said, adding, "Max had business in town, and he may be a little late."

"Never you mind," Ardenia responded. "The food is still warm."

"Major Devonshire and Colonel Beacham are somewhat concerned about the upcoming trip to Bellingfast Estates, just as we all are."

Ardenia closed the door, and the two ladies headed toward the dinner table. Two men stood up as Clarice and Constance were seated at the oblong table. Immediately, two butlers came in and prepared to served the guests. Just as they began, Max entered the room and found his place at the table next to Clarice.

Major Devonshire spoke up first. "Lady Lindsey, you are well aware of the purpose of our visit here today, are you not?"

"I rather expected you to call before we made the trip," she replied.

"We just couldn't put it off any longer," Colonel Beacham added. "We have contacted Scotland Yard several times, and each conversation has disturbed us greatly. There have been five unexplainable deaths in the past two years. One cannot conclude if the deaths were suicide or homicide."

Quickly, Eunice Clarice spoke up. "Enough of that nonsense! Enough! Enough! Not another word."

Major Devonshire then stood up and said, "Mrs. Herrington we have important matters to discuss, and you will hear us out."

Eunice Clarice agreed, saying, "It won't matter, but go ahead."

Colonel Beacham chimed in. "Sir Ian Blair sent to us the commissioner's report from the last three-year period. All these individual deaths occurred while these people were attending Madam MaRooska's exclusive resort. I am not permitted to grant you the names, only the details. Two wealthy stockbrokers from Australia were on a boating excursion. The men came up missing. The boat was never recovered, and the men simply disappeared.

"A rich heiress was murdered while attending the horse races at Londonberry Estates. After the race was over the young woman was unexplainably trampled by the winning horse, Super Sleuth. All her winnings from the purse money went to her brother. Both people were famous diplomats from Amsterdam. Nothing was ever done, and the murder is still unsolved. Madam MaRooska denied any involvement in the incident, and the commissioner's investigation came to a halt. Yes, this is another unsolved mystery at Madam MaRooska's exclusive resort.

"The last two deaths were individuals from the United States. This was a couple from Brownsville, Vermont. It was reported that they died in a car crash, as they were headed for Bangor, Ireland."

Major Devonshire stood up again and took the floor. "We highly suggest that you all cancel your reservations at once. It is too dangerous to attend any of her events in Ireland, especially the fall events. Most of the deaths have occurred during the fall events."

"Our reservations are in, and they have been confirmed," Lady Lindsey said, adding with adamancy, "We will be attending this event."

Then Eunice Clarice interrupted. "My daughter is an author. She has several chapters to conclude at the end of her book. We have all agreed that on her behalf she must return to Bellingfast Estates to finish the concluding chapters at Madam MaRooska's Specialty Resort."

At that, Eunice Clarice stood up. "If you all will excuse me, my husband and I have business matters to discuss.

We will be leaving for Paris very soon. Come on, Mac."

The two of them left the dining room and went upstairs.

Major Davenport and Colonel Beacham looked puzzled at each other.

"Well..." Major Devonport said and then sighed. "I guess there is nothing else to say."

"Precisely right," Lady Lindsey responded.

Major Davenport and Colonel Beacham stood up. Ardenia walked in from the kitchen entrance.

"Ardenia..." Lady Lindsey said. "These men have completed their work for today. Please escort them out."

Ardenia obliged, escorting the two gentlemen to the front door. They promptly drove away.

•••

Lady Lindsey and Constance arrived at the Louis Armstrong International Airport in New Orleans. The plane was scheduled to take off at 5 PM. They had already printed their boarding passes and were in line to board the plane, chatting to each other.

Constance says, "I am very excited about being with Virginia Camille."

"Yes," Lady Lindsey replied. "You girls have always been close. You are about the same age, I presume."

"Yes, Virginia Camille is a couple of years older than I am. But yes, you are right. We have always been close."

"Why, I can remember the summers you two spent with me at Parkview Plantation," Lady Lindsey reminisced. "Aunt Glenora was living with me during those happy times. We did cherish the times you girls spent with us."

"We only had a month and a half in the summertime because Mama always wanted me to be with her before I went back to school," Constance explained. "Yes, I did enjoy being with Mac and Mama, but those summer days at Parkview with Virginia Camille, Aunt Glenora, and you were the best overall. No doubt about it; they were the best."

"You all scared us to death," Lady Lindsey explained.

"When? When? What did we do?" Constance inquired.

"Well, as I recollect...Virginia Camille had just gotten her driver's license."

"I remember now!" Candance broke in. "She wanted to drive the limo to town. We were going to the soda fountain to have an ice cream sundae."

"Yes, Aunt Glenora and I both agreed it was all right," Lady Lindsey interjected. "But you all had to be back with an hour or so."

"Well, I tried to convince Virginia Camille to just do what you said, but you know my cousin. She has a one-track mind, and it is hard to persuade her once she has made up her mind. Anyway, we took the old back county road toward the river. Virginia Camille was not worried. She knew she would have plenty of time in the two-hour span to get back home.

"There was an old dirt road that ran right along the river. I knew the road was too narrow, and we did not need to be squeezing into that small space. I tried again to tell her that the road was too narrow. She did not hear a word I said. We drove slowly up the old river road. Virginia Camille suggested that we get out for a while and dabble in the creek. I was very reluctant, but Virginia Camille was already out of the car, sitting on the bank with her toes dangling in the water.

"So, I followed. We sat there about thirty minutes. Then I suggested it was time to go back home. She let me know that we still had plenty of time. When we got back to the car, it hit us that there was no place to turn the big limo around. I inquired as to what we were going to do. We thought a minute. There was a bare spot on the road. Virginia Camille slowly backed the limo toward the bare spot. She quickly turned the wheel and proceeded to put her foot on the gas.

"Lo and behold, she hit a huge tree in the middle of the bare space. The car made a huge impact. We knew the limo had been damaged. There was no way we could turn the limo around. I asked her what we would do next. She suggested that we would wait for them to find us. They did, and it was five hours later, when the Bastrop, Louisiana police found us. The tow truck carried the limo to the body shop to be repaired."

"Let me tell you..." Lady Lindsey said. "Her father was furious. He made all kinds of threats, but I'm sure he didn't follow through on any of them."

The airline pilot made his final announcement. "Please buckle your seatbelt. We will be landing at the Atlanta Hartfield International Airport in a few minutes. Put your tray tables up. Those going to Phoenix, go to Terminal A, gate 14. Those going to Philadelphia will go to a Terminal F, gate 16, and those going to New York will exit to Terminal G, gate 2. If Atlanta is your destination, welcome to the Peach State. The weather is clear with a temperature of 79 degrees. Enjoy your stay, and please fly with Delta again."

Lady Lindsey and Constance got off the plane. They were excited. They made their way through the airport to the shuttle that would take them to Terminal G.

"I anticipate that Virginia Camille will already be at gate 2," said Lady Lindsey.

"I hope so," Constance replied. "We only have one hour before we board the plane."

Lady Lindsey, Virginia Camille, and Constance were seated in first class on an Air France flight to Dublin, Ireland.

"It's going to be a long ride, girls," Lady Lindsey advised them. "Sit back and relax. Plug in your earphones and read a good book. This will make the trip to Dublin go faster."

Throughout their flight, Virginia Camille began to quiz Constance on her last trip to Bellingfast Estates.

"Well, the whole area is beautiful," Constance admitted. "Bellingfast Estates is an old Abbey built in the early 1800's. It looks like an old English Castle. Madam MaRooska has two events each year. Many of the guests had signed up years in advance to guarantee a reservation. The most prominent and influential people from around the globe are invited to attend. Famous painters, world-known musicians, philosophers, celebrities, and politicians frequent the halls of the Abbey."

Virginia Camille inquired, "Why did you go to Bellingfast in the first place?"

"It's a long story. My novel was almost complete. I only had a few more chapters to finish. Lady Lindsey thought I could be exposed to some world-famous novelist. Possibly by being around these influential people, I could get some suggestions and insights on how to complete my novel."

"Lady Lindsey said that you have several publishers competing to publish your book," Virginia Camille interjected.

"I do, but if you recall, I never finished the book," Constance said, explaining, "The experience at Bellingfast was so horrible that I had a complete nervous breakdown. I'm just now getting the courage to start writing again."

"So...why are we going back to the Castle?" Virginia Camille asked.

"All the experts in journalism say I must go back and face these demons, so I can continue in the field of journalism. If I give up now, I will never write again. I'll be scared to share these historical events."

Virginia Camille listened attentively, but not being a writer herself, she really did not understand what Constance was trying to explain. "Oh well."

Virginia Camille plugged in the earphones and continued to read a book. After leaving JFK International Airport, the plane followed the usual route, traveling up the East Coast to Newfoundland and then crossing the North Atlantic Ocean straight to Ireland. Eight hours later, the plane landed in Dublin, Ireland, at the Collinstown Airport. There, the three boarded a small aircraft to Belfast, Ireland.

Madam MaRooska was in her office making sure that all last-minute details for the two-week extravaganza were in place. The guests would begin arriving in the next few hours. She wanted to be sure of all the last-minute details and arrangements were in perfect order. James, MaRooska's personal advisor, was explaining them to her.

"Madam, the phone has been ringing off the hook." James said fretfully. "These investors are trying their best to break in again."

"Now, James..." Madam MaRooska said. "You know it is our tradition and custom to never engage in international business profits or endeavors until our guests have been properly served. Tomorrow is the masquerade ball, and I do not want anything to go wrong."

"I must ask you again, did you check each briefing carefully?" James asked. "You remember last year."

Madam MaRooska admitted, "Yes, I checked. The unfortunate mishap last year cost Lord Tutwiller over a quarter of a million pounds, and poor Senor Gonzales... it cost him his life. I have checked this situation over, and it will not happen like that again."

"Let me get on back to the main desk. I'm sure Sir Callahan and Sir Richardson will need my assistance as the guest arrive."

"Oh!" Madam MaRooska remembered something. "Did the costume for Ann Boleyn ever arrive? Last year, it so was irreparably damaged that they had to send it to London for repairs. I know it had to be repaired."

"Yes, ma'am," James answered. "The curiosity shop was pleased with the excellent seamstress and repair work. The seamstress from London took our sketches and redid the gown with exquisite taste. I am sure you will be pleased. Now, excuse me, while I go on downstairs."

Chapter 2

Arrival at Bellingfast

The deboarding process was swift, and the three ladies descended the few stairs off the plane and made their way to the car waiting for them.

"There's Madam MaRooska's famous resort!" Lady Lindsey exclaimed, pointing at the side of the car, which was covered in a painting of the resort.

The limo driver escorted the three ladies to the limousine and put their luggage into the back, and they headed for Bellingfast Estates. As they approached Bellingfast Estates, the two-mile winding road gave a full view of the magnificent Chateau Fort. The castle had been converted into an abbey and was used as a resort for the rich and famous. The four-story stone house was surrounded by mountains and a rolling vale with a perfectly manicured countryside. The old abbey was a masterpiece of design. There were two large towers, ten pitched roofs, and five gables with elaborate ornamentation on the exterior of the building. As the limo pulled up to the door, two men in black jackets approached it. One man opened the door, and the other instructed the driver to help him take the luggage to the side entrance where all luggage was disbursed.

As Constance, Lady Lindsey, and Virginia Camille walked toward the front entrance, two extremely wide doors opened. As they walked through the limestone arches and on to the polished marble floors, they marveled at the impressive entrance hall. This was the garden hallway. This hall gave all the visitors a place to relax as they enjoyed the exotic plants and marble and bronze sculptures. Chairs and tables were scattered throughout the room. Many of the guests had already arrived and begun to mix and mingle with each other.

In the southwest corner of the room was a heavily carved desk that was made from walnut. The desk was in the Grand Baroque style, and it was about ten feet long. On the wall above the desk were individual, locked panels. These panels held the room keys for each of the guests visiting the resort.

As the ladies walked toward the long desk, they observed two men, dressed in black. They were standing behind the table. One stood on each end.

The man with a dark mustache addressed the ladies first, saying, "Lady Lindsey and Stalling girls."

"Yes," Lady Lindsey answered.

"I am Sir Richardson, and the other gentleman is Sir Callahan."

Sir Richardson chimed in. "Your luggage has been sent up to the second floor. You ladies have adjoining rooms. You are to collect your keys, go to your rooms, and then join the rest of the group in the Grand Hall in the Garden Room."

The phone rang, and Sir Callahan answered. "Yes, madam, they have just arrived."

Meanwhile, Sir Richardson opened boxes 201 and 202, retrieved two envelopes, and handed the ladies each an envelope that corresponded with their respective rooms. Room 202 had two keys, meaning that Constance and Virginia Camille would room together while Lady Lindsey had a room of her own.

The ladies took the envelopes and got the keys as they proceeded to their rooms. They walked back through the Grand Hall to a winding staircase that led to the second floor. Glancing throughout the Grand Hall, Virginia Camille was extremely impressed with the clientele. She could tell these were very distinguished people. She noticed their expensive apparel and exquisite jewelry and accessories. One would have to admit that only the rich and famous would be accepted as guests to this type of affair.

Upon entering room 202, it was obvious that their suitcases had been opened. Their clothes were lying on the bed. All their jewelry and accessories had been placed on the dresser. There were two marble-topped commodes from an early French period. The two chairs were Louis XV. Two double beds in French provincial matched the marble-topped commodes.

"Well..." Virginia Camille was astonished. "I never expected anything as elaborate as this."

"Don't let this place fool you," Constance answered. "Mark my word. They are watching every move you make."

There was a knock at the door. It was Lady Lindsey. She had the adjoining room to the girls.

"Are you girls ready to go down?" she asked.

"No," Constance answered. "Let us freshen up a bit."

The two girls went into the salon. When they came out, all three of the ladies headed down the long winding staircase to the Grand Hall to meet the other guests. When they arrived in the entrance hall, all the guests had moved into the Garden Room, which adjoined the entrance hall.

Once in the Garden Room, they saw that all the guests were already seated at a circular table. There were exotic plants all around and rattan and bamboo furniture. There were three vacant chairs, with three gold nameplates in front of the chairs. Sir Richardson escorted the three ladies to their chairs and assisted them as they took their places at the table.

Everything was incredibly quiet.

Then a loud bong was heard. After the bong stopped, everybody knew that Madam MaRooska was about to enter the room from a side entrance with maroon curtains. The curtains extended up twelve feet to the dome-shaped archway. The Madam came through the maroon velvet draperies, walked straight toward the circular tables, and positioned herself in the middle of the tables.

There was a massive oak table about three feet tall with a width of seven feet. The Madam stepped up onto the table. This was a sign that her first address was about to begin.

"Distinguished guests, we here at Madam MaRooska's Specialty Resort are very honored to have you join us for this spectacular occasion. I realize some of you have been on our guest reservation list for two years. Several of the guests have been here before. You enjoyed the events so much that you decided to come back and join us again. This year's event has somewhat changed. The costume get-acquainted party will start at noon tomorrow and end at midnight. Information packets are placed in front of each participant. Read over your packet thoroughly. After the dinner, the limos will be running all night, making trips to and from the costume shop. Dressmakers and seamstresses will be on hand for all alterations. Are there any questions?"

One elderly lady spoke up. "I really do not understand what you mean by the costume party."

Madam MaRooska responded, "All the details are explained in your customized, selective packet. Again, read it carefully. If that is all..."

She paused for any other questions to be asked. No one offered any up, so she continued. "Enjoy your meal. My staff is ready to serve you."

The butler's staff then began to server the dinner and drinks. The guests all seemed to enjoy the meal. At the conclusion of the elaborate dinner, the guests began to get up. Some of the guests went up the stairs and took the elevators to their assigned rooms. Other guests meandered around back to the grand entrance hall. However, all guests had their reservation packets in hand. Some guests were studying the information as they walked around. Others sat on the plush chairs to study the directions in more detail.

Virginia Camille then questioned Constance. "What do we do now?"

Lady Lindsey spoke up quickly. "Girls, I feel we'd best do as Madam MaRooska said. We need to go immediately to the costume shop and choose our gowns and apparel."

As the ladies walked outside the building, the limos were lined up around the winding driveway. Two groups of guests were already in line. When those guests departed, the next limo driver opened the doors for Lady Lindsey, Constance, and Virginia Camille. The three of them went on their way to the costume shop.

Lady Lindsey again tried to give helpful instructions. "Girls, be reading your packets. You need to have an idea of which character you'd like to portray at the party."

"But be careful," said Constance. "The character you choose will become your destiny. The events you will experience will be the same type of events your character had to face. Be incredibly careful. The glamorous aristocratic and celebrity characters face many trials and tribulations, and you too will have to face these same obstacles as you complete your two-week stay at Bellingfast Estates."

"Can our selections bring danger to us?" Virginia Camille asked.

"They could," Constance responded.

"I am not worried one bit," Lady Lindsey encouraged the girls. "You girls are smart and level-headed. I am sure you all will be quite capable of making the right choices in every encounter and endeavor."

"I hope so," Virginia Camille stated uncertainly. "There are a lot of interesting people here at this resort, and I do not want to get involved with the wrong type of gentleman."

Twenty minutes later, the limo arrived at the costume shop. The costume shop was an old building, constructed on the side of a cliff that was overhanging the North Channel. The old building had three levels. The first level was a bookstore called The Curiosity Shop. The second level was the costume shop. The owner lived on the third level.

People from Northern Ireland were awfully familiar with the old building. The bookstore and costume shop were extremely popular. People of all ages enjoyed browsing these two levels. The costume shop became increasingly active when Madam MaRooska hired seamstresses and tailors to custom size her guests at the resort.

The bottom level was entered on the ground level, but to get to the costume shop, one had to walk the outside stairs up to the second level. This place of business was made of clay and brick and had a thatched roof. When Lady Lindsey, Constance, and Virginia Camille got out of the limo, they saw several other guests walking up the outside stairs to the second-floor level. Stepping inside the shop, you could see that this was a terribly busy place. Rows and rows of costumes hung throughout the shop.

"Let us browse around before we choose which of the costumes we actually want," Virginia Camille suggested. "Look at this beautiful gown."

The owner of the boutique walked over to Virginia Camille as she and Lady Lindsey admired the beautiful gown. "That's an exact replica of the gown Grace Kelly wore in her wedding to the Prince Rainier III of Monaco, It is an exquisite gown. If you desire this one, it can be altered within a short period of time."

"Well, I haven't decided yet which character I will portray," Virginia Camille responded.

The owner of the shop nodded and then walked away to help another customer.

Virginia noticed two very nice-looking gentlemen costumes, representative of early Ireland. She made a point to stand near the men so that she could hear the conversation in which they were involved. The larger man kept referring to Finn McCool and what a great hero he was.

The smaller man remarked, "He was kind of like King Arthur. I am very interested in Brian Bord, Ireland's hero and high king. His costume is so elaborate."

The larger man said, "The gems and gold that lace the wardrobe are beyond compare."

"Precisely," the smaller man stated. "I could feel quite at ease wearing these clothes and playing this part."

Virginia Camille was impressed with the men, so she tried to memorize what they looked like and what the costumes looked like. She knew that she would get acquainted with these men at the costume ball.

Meanwhile, Constance was incredibly careful in her selection. She was going to choose a character who was very plain and quiet. Constance did not want to be in the spotlight, and she wanted to be sure her character had not had any traumatic experience in her lifetime. Constance was interested in the Bronte sisters. The Bronte sisters were a literary family from the village of Haworth.

"Constance," Lady Lindsey addressed her. "I have made my decision on which character I'll portray."

As Constance walked toward Lady Lindsey, she could see the costume spoke for itself.

"Why, I recognize the costume," Constance remarked. "You're going to be Catherine the Great."

"Have you made your choice?" Lady Lindsey asked.

"Not yet, but I have two choices in mind. I cannot decide. I am extremely interested in Jacqueline Onassis or Princess Diana. I will probably choose Jacqueline Onassis over Princess Diana. Diana's tragic death was so horrendous, and I do not know if I want to go through all those stressful emotions. I have also been considering one of the literary writers or the one of the Bronte sisters." She spotted her aunt and said, "Oh, there is Virginia Camille, I think I will get her opinion."

As Virginia approached the two ladies, both Lady Lindsey and Constance were astonished. It was quite apparent that Virginia Camille would be representing the famous movie star Marilyn Monroe.

"The dress is beautiful," Constance noted.

The dress was quite recognizable. It was the white dress that Marilyn wore when the wind blew the dress high enough to see her panties.

"You could not have made a better decision," Lady Lindsey commented, "The choice is so like you. I know you will certainly enjoy playing that part at the get-acquainted party."

Then Constance told Virginia Camille about the characters she wanted to portray.

Virginia Camille did not hesitate to offer her advice. "Be Jacqueline Onassis. She is such an elegant woman."

With the approval of Virginia Camille, Constance chose Jacqueline Onassis. The three ladies took the dresses to the fitting room to have them adjusted for the upcoming costume party and ball.

Chapter 3

The Masquerade Ball

The next day's excitement was in the air. Everybody at Madam MaRooska's Bellingfast Estates was getting ready for the upcoming event. The events were to begin at noon. All the guests had been to the costume shop. They had picked out and been fitted for the characters they chose to portray.

The first activity was the most important activity for the next two weeks. Each guest had been given specific assignments and tasks that they were to complete during the next twelve-hour span. The information gathered at the get-acquainted party and the masquerade ball was essential to ensure an enjoyable, informative, and safe two-week stay at Bellingfast Estates.

As directed by Madam MaRooska, the guests began to enter the ballroom.

The ballroom was the largest room in the house. It measured seventy-two feet long and forty-five feet wide, with a forty-foot-tall vaulted ceiling. Special furniture had been designed for the room. Two build-in gilt-trimmed throne chairs, an oak dining table, and fifty chairs made up the decor. There was a triple fireplace flanked with armor dating from the 1400s to the 1800s. Above the mantle was a high relief panel entitled, "The Return of the Chase". There was another built-in sideboard showcasing 18th and 19th century brass and copper vessels from England, Holland, and Spain.

As the guests gathered around the extraordinary room, they were astonished. The incredibly intricate detail of the ornate plasterwork ceiling, the Italian marble wainscoting, and the door trim were breathtaking. Truly, when one entered this room, it was evident that royalty was in the air. The guests were dressed in the outfits they had chosen at the costume shop. It was very strange, Constance thought, because as the guests entered through the east wing, they had to stop by the restored organ and pick up the masks that were assigned for their outfits. Sir Richardson and Sir Callahan were at the organ. As the guest came in, it was obvious that the men know exactly which mask went with which costume. Virginia Camille was disgusted. She had spent an hour getting her hair fixed right, and now had to pull the mask over her hair and face. Yes, she was distraught over the whole matter.

After all the guests had entered the room, the organ began to play. The music was unbelievably soft and a little mysterious. Again, Constance remembered being there several years earlier. She remembered that the lavish costumes, scenery, and music were the same. However, the guests were not required to wear the masks before.

How strange, she thought. If one could not identify the characters by their costumes, then conversation would be quite important.

Smoking his pipe and standing next to two gentlemen at the library entrance, a small-framed man with silver and gray streaked hair was looking around the room. The man was very polished looking. He was from Wellington Estates in New Zealand. New Zealand was home to a busy seaport founded in 1865 by the New Zealand Trading Company. His home in New Zealand was on a 1500-acre estate. It was a beautiful estate for the Wellington families. Doctor Wellington had visited Madam MaRooska's exquisite tours twice before. He always found them quite exciting.

The charming visitors were always so well-matched. One would believe that the Madam was a goddess herself because of her tremendous talent of matching their personalities. Doctor Wellington had met several worthy aristocratic debutantes, but he always enjoyed playing the field with these interesting females. He would meet the ladies interested in him, then he would mysteriously disappear into another pursuit.

One man turned toward Doctor Wellington and introduced himself. "I'm Robert L. Hightower." He offered to shake his hand. "I've been observing you in the billiard room. I gather you've been here quite often."

Doctor Wellington responded, "Well, yes, I've been a guest on several occasions."

"Well, what can I expect from attending this magnificent event?"

Dr. Wellington looked very sternly at the man. "What are you looking for?"

"I've had my name on the waiting list for two years. I have contacted several participants from around the world. Some of the participants came for the tour, but some did not. However, I was amazed that most of the parties said truly very little about the visit at Bellingfast, and I got the distinct impression that they seemed to think I was actually invading their privacy by even asking."

"You probably were, and you are quite right. These tours are very selective. If you stay for the entire event, I assure you, I doubt you will have much to say either. Excuse me...what is your name again?"

"Robert Hightower," he repeated.

"Nice to meet you, Robert," said Doctor Wellington. "I must leave. I have got a client to see. I will be bringing her to the masquerade ball." Then Dr. Wellington abruptly left the ballroom and got into a limousine out front. The third gentleman was left standing, as Dr. Wellington and Robert departed.

Sir Callahan approached the gentleman and asked, "Would you care for more hors d'oeuvres? They are very tasty."

Robert Hightower walked back into the dining hall. Several of the guests were seated at small tables. There was also a long buffet table where the guests could serve themselves. Two ladies were seated at one of the small tables. Robert introduced himself, and the ladies asked him to join them. The three guests were seated at the small table in the middle of the room. One guest was dressed as Cleopatra or Sophia Loren, and the other lady guest was Madam Curie. The distinguished gentleman who introduced himself as Robert was dressed as the Arch Bishop of Canterbury. With the mask covering their faces, you had to visualize what the actual person looked like.

One of the ladies introduced herself as the Governor of Arizona, and the other lady explained that she was an actress. Robert Hightower then excused himself and went to the big table. He took a plate from the buffet back to the small round table and began to enjoy the food he had picked out.

As the guests continued to socialize, they shared abstract details of their personal lives. One of the ladies explained that her costume represented Madam Curie.

Robert then spoke up. "She was a Polish and French chemist, wasn't she?"

"Yes," the lady dressed as Cleopatra added. "She conducted pioneer research on radioactivity. She discovered radium."

The lady dressed as Cleopatra addressed the gentleman. "And who might you be?"

"I'm Sir Hightower from Luxemburg," Robert eagerly explained. "I've been on the waiting list for two years. Is this your first visit to Madam MaRooska's Specialty Resort?"

Both ladies nodded.

"I am from America," the lady dressed as Cleopatra remarked. "And I am an actress."

"Oh, how nice." Sir Hightower grinned. "So you are a real celebrity, I presume?"

The three guests continued to chat for a while. Then, losing interest, Sir Hightower decided to move on and mingle with some more of the guests.

Sir Callahan was talking with Mrs. Hatfield.

"I really don't know why Mr. Wellington keeps returning to Bellingfast Estate."

"Yes," Mrs. Hatfield replied. "We all know that each time a guest returns for a visit, the registration fee triples."

"We are aware of that fact," Sir Callahan interrupted. "However, undoubtedly he must have much more money than we anticipated and much more time for him to come here two times in one year."

Mrs. Hatfield had calculated the enormous sum that he had spent thus far.

"He appears to be so thin," Sir Callahan remarked. "I wonder if he is ill."

"Well, as a matter of fact..." Mrs. Hatfield addressed the concern. "His chef did wire in a special diet. Looks like he has gastroenteritis or some type of stomach disorder. I'm sure I'll have to make special instructions available to the chef, as they prepare his dishes. We cannot afford to make him sicker than he is. He is way too thin as it is."

"I overheard him make a remark about picking up a certain client whom he wanted to meet."

"Oh, yes," Mrs. Hatfield interjected. "He's picking the woman up. You remember, she is the executive with IBM from Italy."

"Oh, yes," Sir Callahan answered. "Her luggage arrived last week. I had to use two rooms in order to store all her belongings. Undoubtedly, she thinks she is going to be staying several months."

"I don't think so," Mrs. Hatfield quickly responded. "Madam MaRooska only had her down for two weeks. Seems like this is her first visit."

Sir Callahan broke in. "That explains it! Those Italians and their wearing apparel."

Lady Lindsey began to gaze around the room, looking for an interesting character to investigate. Naturally, being an elderly woman, her immediate attention was drawn toward elderly gentlemen. Looking toward the triple fireplace, a very distinguished, silver-haired man was standing and smoking a pipe. He was dressed in a Roman costume made from wool cloth. He also had on a sleeveless tunic. Being a character from ancient Rome, he was adorned with gemstone jewelry and golden rings. Yes, Lady Lindsey did feel inspired to make his acquaintance. As she approached him, he made an about face and walked toward Catherine the Great. He took her hand and kissed it. Then he bowed down in front of her.

Lady Lindsey was surprised, and she curtsied back to him.

"Julius Caesar, I presume?" Lady Lindsey acknowledged his acquaintance in correct style.

"Is this your first trip to Bellingfast Estates?" he precociously inquired.

"Yes, it is. Madam MaRooska and I are longtime friends. We have mutual friends in New York, and we have been at several sorority events over the years. However, this is the first time for me to come to her villa."

"I do hope you enjoy your visit."

Then the man in the Julius Caesar costume made an abrupt departure.

Well, Lady Lindsey thought to herself. I didn't even get his name.

The stage was set and in walked Henry VIII and Anne Boleyn. Doctor Charles Wellington, a wealthy landowner in his forties or fifties was a perfect match for Anne Boleyn, who was a business IBM executive from Italy. Doctor Wellington had come to the ball early but had to make an abrupt exit to take the limo to pick up Miss Ramona. She was still at the costume shop getting her gown altered. She was late getting her gown, and Doctor Wellington agreed to pick her up. All the other guests had arrived. When Henry VIII and Anne Boleyn entered together, a small orchestra began to play.

The instructions had been given in the information packet. Each female guest had been paired with a male guest. When the orchestra began, the individual character was to try to locate his or her match from the information packet and dance with them.

Lady Lindsey, Constance, and Virginia Camille were gathered around a sideboard, showcasing the vessels from Spain and England. As they were standing there, the three ladies were discussing the information included in the packet. The packet included the physical characteristics of the partner each female was to try to locate.

"Well, they have pretty well eliminated my opportunities," Lady Lindsey remarked.

"What do you mean?" Constance asked. "I'm to be paired with an elderly gentleman somewhere between the ages of 60 to 80."

"However, the packet did say that the gentleman is very distinct," Lady Lindsey replied.

"Oh, don't be so pessimistic," Virginia Camille interjected. "You could end up with a jewel! Now let me see." Virginia read her packet instructions. "What and who am I looking for? I just hope he is not a little creep with a lot of money. It says I am paired with a wealthy landowner from New Zealand. Wealthy is a good adjective, but personality and good looks certainly play a part in this scenario."

Lady Lindsey turned to Constance. "And what does it say about your gentleman?"

"Not much," Constance answered. "Except this is his first visit to Bellingfast, and he is an author and a lawyer."

"How quaint," Lady Lindsey remarked. "I'm sure you all will get along quite well."

"I hope so," Constance replied.

As the orchestra played, the ladies began to browse around, hoping to find the match that was indicated on the instruction sheet.

Virginia Camille was flaunting herself around the ballroom, and she was flirting with all the men in sight. Her long blond hair and the Marilyn Monroe gown that she had chosen were quite eye-catching. Young men and older men all hoped she would be their catch. It really did not matter who Virginia Camille was paired with; she knew she would have her pick before the night was over, no matter who the gentleman was assigned to be with. Virginia Camille was beginning to genuinely enjoy herself.

When Madam MaRooska spied Lady Lindsey, she immediately went to her side and took her by the hand.

"Lady Lindsey," Madam MaRooska acknowledged her presence. "I was thrilled when I found out you were going to make this event. I suppose it's been several years since I saw you in Manhattan. My, how long it's been."

"Well, over three years," Lady Lindsey said. "I have been in the hospital and could not attend the last concerto that you sponsored. However, when I found out about this year's Bellingfast spring event in Ireland, I was determined to make the voyage. I'm here with my niece and granddaughter."

"I'm sure you all will have a fantastic time," Madam MaRooska assured her. "By the way, did Constance ever finish her novel?"

"Not yet, Madam MaRooska," Lady Lindsey explained. "That's why we all encouraged her to return to

Bellingfast and finish the last three chapters."

"Fantastic!" Madam MaRooska exclaimed. "I am looking forward to visiting with you all during your visit here at Bellingfast Estates."

Two men were secretly whispering to each other in one corner of the ballroom. Both men appeared to be around fifty or so. One was dressed as Czar Nicholas, and the other was dressed as Lawrence of Arabia. Captain Nathaniel Wright was dressed as Henry Kissinger.

He approached the gentlemen and inquired, "Are you gentlemen business associates of Lord Tutwiller?"

The taller man, dressed as Czar Nicholas, quickly responded, "You might say so." Then he tried to change the subject and commented, "Lovely party, lovely party. I think I'll get myself another glass of Sherry."

The persistent Henry Kissinger asked, "What is the best stock recommended by your company?"

Sir Ralph Grantly Adams III reluctantly answered, "Our brokers are always encouraged to go with Blue Chip."

"Excuse us, sir," the shorter man interrupted. He grabbed his brother by the elbow and quickly rushed him out of the ballroom and into the billiard room.

Sir Ralph Grantly Adams III asked his brother, "Did you get the jewels?"

Sir Reggie Adams took the beaded purse out of his coat pocket and whispered, "Yes, I cleaned her out."

"What about the account?"

"I cleaned the account out," Sir Reggie explained. "I switched the funds right into the Angel Doll account."

Sir Ralph was shocked and amazed that the transaction was made so quickly. Sir Reggie opened the beaded purse, and the two men were gazing at the extravagant jewels when in walked Sissily. Sissily was hired by Madam MaRooska. Startled, the men knew they were not supposed to be in the billiard room at this specific time.

"Can I be of assistance to you gentlemen?" Sissily asked.

Sissily was hired as a housemaid. She was of striking Nigerian descent. She had been with the Madam for several years. Sissily worked closely with Miss Hatfield, another negro consultant for Madam MaRooska. These two women were aware of everything that went on Bellingfast Estates, as well as being remarkably familiar with the events that went on at Lord Tutwiller's neighboring estate, Londonberry Estate.

"No assistance needed," Sir Ralph Adams said and quickly added, "We'll just get on back to the costume ball."

The two men hastened to make a fast exit.

Meanwhile, Virginia Camille was still making the rounds. She had made bodily contact with five of the gentlemen at the ball. The orchestra had stopped for intermission. Lady Lindsey, Constance, and Virginia Camille were in the powder room, waiting to use the toilet.

"Have you all had fun?" Lady Lindsey asked the girls.

Virginia Camille was quick to answer. "Yes, I have, but to my disappointment, Doctor Charles Wellington has turned out to be a bit of a bore. He is a wealthy landowner from New Zealand. He is incredibly attractive but nowhere as interesting as the Barbados twins."

"Oh, you beware of those men," Constance warned. "I think they may be imposters."

"What?!" Virginia Camille questioned. "What do you mean by imposters?"

Lady Lindsey then spoke up. "Lord Tutwiller made mention that Madam MaRooska was very leery when those young men submitted their application to attend the spring event. Lord Tutwiller said the references in their personal biographies and the personality contact resource came back blank. However, when a personal check arrived from their uncle, who was Ambassodor from Barbados, Madam MaRooska agreed to let them attend the event."

"How interesting, how interesting..." Virginia Camille was intrigued to hear about all the details concerning the Barbados twins. It made her more anxious to get to know these men and get personally involved with them.

"You'd better be careful," Constance warned her.

Chapter 4

Post Ball Events

The next morning, Madam MaRooska's private chef James was serving the Madam her breakfast in her private dining room.

"Madam MaRooska, I do believe your assumption is correct," James admitted.

"What do you mean, James?" Madam MaRooska inquired.

"Well..." he began. "The guests from Barbados are intolerable gentlemen, and I am sure they are legitimate imposters."

"What has driven you to make such an accusation?" Madam MaRooska asked.

"Several weeks ago, I was in the servant's dining hall. Several messages came through on the telephone in the servant's quarters. I was not concerned at the time because we have all kinds of strange messages left with us concerning the guests."

The phone rang, and Gertrude answered. "This is Madam MaRooska's Specialty Resort." Alarmed by the remarks made on the phone, Gertrude began to question the caller, "What? What? Who? Now, say that again!"

Sissily heard all the talk and commotion that Gertrude was causing. Gertrude was trying to get information over the phone from the caller.

Sissily firmly spoke up to reprimand Gertrude. "Madam MaRooska specifically told you to never inquire in the personal files of these people, and this could cause you to lose your job! I won't have any part in this. The client's personal lives are confidential. My employment was too important. I want to be left out of the conversation."

Gertrude continued to chatter on the telephone. Gertrude informed Sissily that one could learn about business transactions, such as information about money being moved from one stockholder to another, by listening to phone conversations and just pushing the right button on the computer. She explained that it was amazingly simple. Illegal, but very simple. Gertrude tried to explain more thoroughly, but Sissily told her she had no idea what she was talking about. She went on with her afternoon assignments. Sissily told Gertrude to get a fill-in from the bridge games that night. She suggested that maybe they needed to cancel the games. Sissily explained that Madam MaRooska had asked for volunteers to work a double shift. They would be going to Londonberry Estates for a large party hosted by Lord Tutwiller.

He could not accommodate such a large party and had requested some of Madam MaRooska's staff. Gertrude told her that she would see her tomorrow morning.

Back up on the second floor in their room, Lady Lindsey, Constance, and Virginia Camille were discussing the events and activities that each had chosen for the day. Constance was overly excited. She had been extremely impressed with Sir Hightower.

"What are you two planning for today?" Virginia Camille questioned her. "I'm sure you will enjoy his company, after all both of you are writers."

"Yes, I do like him, and he is an excellent tennis player. We will be spending most of the morning on the tennis courts. What are your plans for today?"

"Doctor Wellington wanted to show me the gardens during the morning hours," Virginia Camille explained.

"How boring, how boring," Constance answered.

"He liked the idea of spending the afternoon playing chess in the library. He likes the privacy and wanted to be alone with me the entire afternoon. I'm sure I'll be busy the rest of my stay with other people and other events here at Bellingfast, so he'd best enjoy the little bit of time I'm going to allow his company. Little does he realize that today may be his only time spent with me!"

"Don't be so rough on the young man, Virginia Camille!" Lady Lindsey reprimanded her. "At least give him a chance."

"Oh, he has had plenty of opportunities to find that special someone! I think he has been attending Madam MaRooska's Specialty Resort for several years. He keeps returning, hoping to find something, but that special something or somebody is beyond my imagination. Oh, well, let me go on downstairs. I'm supposed to meet him at the reception desk to start our exciting day."

As Virginia Camille made her way to the reception desk, Doctor Wellington saw her coming and ventured out to meet her. Kissing her neck, he whispered, "Did you sleep well, my dear?"

"Quite well," she responded. "Just looking forward to this extraordinary day with the debonair Doctor Charles Wellington."

He smiled at her complimentary statement. She took his arm, and he escorted her out the front entrance of Bellingfast Estates. They stepped off the main steps, and a vintage carriage with a driver pulled up. The driver helped Virginia Camille into her seat, and she and Dr. Wellington were off. The forty acres of manicured gardens and grounds complimented the architecture of the estate. The estate included miles of scenic carriage drives, lakes and ponds, and beautiful forests. Doctor Wellington had made this carriage ride so many times that he could recite from memory all the details of the garden ride. As they began to drive through the gardens, Doctor Wellington took Virginia Camille's hand and held it close as he talked to her.

He began to talk in a whisper. "The rich forest covers most of the estate. You will notice that as we travel along the trails, we can see how the forest is transformed into magnificent flower gardens." As Dr. Wellington talked, he began to rub Virginia Camille's hand, caressing her palms and closing his eyes as he talked.

Virginia Camille knew almost immediately that this fellow was a little on the kooky side.

The carriage ride continued, and he pointed out the pansy gardens. "You can see..." he began to explain. "... how the trailing pansies are intermingled with the trailing ivy."

Ten minutes went by. Doctor Wellington stood up and told the driver to stop. The carriage stopped, and Doctor Wellington said, "I want you to see this particular garden. It is my favorite."

Doctor Wellington got off the carriage and pointed to the variegated Japanese laurel.

Then he asked Virginia Camille about the exotic garden. "Just give me your intuitive impression?"

"Well, frankly, I do not know what to say," she replied. "I have toured the Shibazakvra at Hitsojiyama Park. I have studied wisteria at Askhikaga Flower Park. My father and I attended the spring and summer flower festivals in Kyohoshi. It was an incredible experience. However, I do not believe the age-old custom that lovers can be predetermined by passions they share regarding the different variety and species they have in common."

"You seem to be quite knowledgeable about Japanese culture," Dr. Wellington observed.

"Chances are, Doctor Wellington, probably a lot more knowledgeable than you would ever expect!"

With the last remark, Doctor Wellington got back into the carriage, and the driver continued the ride throughout the rest of the gardens. Doctor Wellington did not hold her hand for the rest of the ride. He did continue to point out the specific gardens as they finished the tour.

"The baby doll begonias are beautiful this time of the year," he said.

"Yes, they are," Virginia Camille answered.

Another five minutes passed, and Doctor Wellington spoke again. "And to finish the tour, you'll enjoy viewing the silver heart brunna and the lovely pyracanth."

When the carriage reached the front of the estate, Doctor Wellington got out of the carriage and respectfully helped Virginia Camille out.

Virginia Camille reached over, kissed Doctor Wellington on his cheek, and smiled. "I'll meet you in the library at 7:00 PM."

Virginia Camille did not wait on Doctor Wellington. She quickly left his side and hurried on into the grand hall, looking for someone or something more exciting. Doctor Wellington stood dumbfounded. He really did not know what to expect.

Later that day, Madam MaRooska and Lady Lindsey were enjoying a light lunch in the breakfast room. This room was less formal than the elaborate dining hall.

"I've met the cute little couple from Louisiana," Madam MaRooska noted. "They were just recently married, and their parents from both sides gave the lucky children a honeymoon to our resort."

Lady Lindsey then remarked, "Reuben Rachard's father is deceased, and his mom lives on the top floor in Lafayette, Louisiana, at the La Beaux Magnolia. Rueben's mother and Virginia Camille's father are related. They are first cousins."

"What is Rueben's mother's name?" Madam MaRooska asked.

"Alisha Christina D'La Chaisson."

"Oh, yes," Madam MaRooska said, seeming to remember something. "The D'La Chaissons are big business entrepreneurs in the export and import business in the Hong Kong and Singapore offices."

"Yes, they are quite wealthy and influential entrepreneurs," Lady Lindsey elaborated. "Especially in the Asian countries."

Lady Lindsey and Madam MaRooska were still chatting about the little young couple from Lafayette when, to their surprise, the young couple walked into the breakfast room. When Lady Lindsey spied them, she motioned and got Reuben's attention.

Reuben addressed Elizabeth Anne, as both were excited about seeing Lady Lindsey.

"Please join us," Madam MaRooska interjected. "We would love to share some time with you all."

"Please, sit down," Lady Lindsey added. "Have you all met Madam MaRooska?"

"We were briefly introduced at The masquerade ball," Reuben answered. "So nice to see you again."

Elizabeth Anne said, "Madam MaRooska, I must admit, I have never attended any event that is as extravagant as this one here at Bellingfast."

"Thank you so much," Madam MaRooska said, acknowledging the compliment. "We do try to make the stay here as intriguing, exciting, and enjoyable as we can since we do not advertise our luxury resort. Only by satisfied guests does the word get out. So, I am quite happy to meet you young people and do hope you enjoy your stay."

The lunch was cut short when Miss Hatfield summoned Madam MaRooska to come to the office for an important phone call.

"I must take this call," Madam MaRooska said. "But I'll chat with you all later."

She got up from the table and went to her office.

The group of guests had been enjoying playing games in the billiard hall for a while when

Elizabeth Anne leaned over to Reuben and said, "I am extremely tired." She and Reuben had spent a large portion of the day at the riding academy.

Elizabeth Anne got dressed and retired for the evening to their bed while Reuben was on the computer checking for details on his business contacts. The phone rang, and Reuben answered. After a thirty-minute conversation, Reuben was quite concerned, but more so he was puzzled.

Elizabeth Anne aroused from her sleep. "Reuben, darling? What was that all about?"

Rueben D'La Chaisson had never been one to worry. He was very laid-back. His family had always been in excellent financial shape. He dressed in only the finest summer suits imported from France, and the family had money coming in from investments into their Caribbean stocks. The dividends came in annually.

Reuben had told Elizabeth Anne on numerous occasions, "Sugar dumpling, if I never worked another day in my life, we could live extravagantly and enjoy life to its fullest."

"Reuben...Reuben...?" Elizabeth Anne got out of bed and went to his desk. She began to inquire again about the phone calls.

"Oh," Reuben answered. "It is only Mama. You know she is always worried that we cannot make ends meet."

"I'm very aware that your mother always has her scouts out looking for a new and different job for you! Reuben, Reuben, talk to me! Just what did your mother say?"

"Sugar, honey, you know I don't work myself tooth and toenail like your only brother does," Rueben tried to reassure her. "Correct me if I am wrong, he has traveled the world over, but he'll never live to enjoy the money he has made."

"Will we ever see the day we can collect?"

Assuring her again, Reuben promised, "Sugar, do not worry your pretty little head off. This is precisely why I wanted a Louisiana doll instead of a Georgia intellectual. Just leave all the financial dividends, recruiting, and adjusting to your commander-in-chief. And, please, Honey doll, the next time your parents or my mother start trying to fill your pretty little head with trivial business matters...simply take those cotton balls you use to take off your makeup and stuff them in your ears."

Little Elizabeth Anne was satisfied. Then she kissed him and whispered, "Reuben, Reuben, you are smart!"

"Enough of that," Reuben snapped playfully. "You need to get on back to bed while I finish my work."

Reuben had given enough explanation to his wife, but he knew this matter was a lot more serious than he shared with her and a lot more serious than he could have ever imagined. He knew his mother had already gone to bed, so he decided to call their financial advisor, who worked with his mother on all business matters.

Reuben dialed the number. "Yes, Yes, I have heard. I knew something had gone wrong... What? Who?"

Charles D. Wolf had always been a special counselor concerning the Chaisson's business endeavors in the United States and abroad.

Charles began to explain the situation to Reuben. "I've known your mother has been quite upset for some time now. The Caribbean stocks had expired and are no longer negotiable. A transaction has been forged, and some illegal documentation resulted in loss of twenty to fifty million in international currency. I am so glad you called. I just got off the phone with Admiral Stallings, and he and I decided it is best not to say a word to your mother at this time. She is upset enough, and she doesn't need to be overly confused about the merger of the two companies."

"Will we have to fold the Singapore office?"

"I don't know, Reuben," Charles said, continuing to explain, "I simply don't know at this time. Irresponsible, deliberate, and unacceptable bidding has us under scrutiny. Stockholders are questioning our credibility. Admiral Stallings seems the least concerned. So many of his funds are tied up with Lady Lindsey's estate. He really does not care what happens."

"Charles, it's getting late. I'll teletype you tomorrow and give you updated details as they come in." Reuben hung up the phone and went to bed.

Constance was in the powder room, brushing her hair and readjusting her tennis outfit. She and Sir Hightower had planned a morning of tennis. In the afternoon, they were going horseback riding on the country trails at Bellingfast Estates. Constance was looking forward to being with Sir Hightower.

The phone rang and Constance picked it up. "Hello? Yes, I'll be right down."

When they arrived at the tennis courts, it was obvious that several couples had planned to play tennis. There were four tennis courts, and two of them were already occupied. When Constance spied the twins from Barbados, she was a little frightened. There had been so many negative remarks about the two men, and Constance did not want to be near them.

"Oh, there are the Barbados twins," Sir Hightower announced. "I enjoyed being with them at the masquerade ball. Why don't we ask them to join us for a game of doubles?"

"I...I...I'd rather not," Constance said. "Let us just play by ourselves."

"Oh, Constance," Sir Hightower said. "I'm sure you will do just fine."

Sir Hightower quickly left Constance's side and approached one of the twins from Barbados. After chatting briefly, Sir Hightower motioned for Constance to come to the court that Countess Christina Anderson and Sir Ralph Adams were playing on. Sir Ralph Adams was a strikingly handsome young man.

When he saw Constance, he hollered to her, "Come on over, Miss Stallings! We would love to have you all play with us."

Reluctantly, Constance slowly walked toward the tennis courts. Countess Christina had already gone to Sir Ralph's side of the court. Sir Hightower grabbed Constance's arm, and the game began. They played several matches. Constance and Sir Hightower won all of them. Sir Hightower was an excellent player. He made practically all the points.

After the third game, Ralph suggested, "Why don't we take a break and try some refreshments at the bar?"

"Excellent idea," Sir Hightower agreed.

As they were going toward the snack bar, Sir Ralph approached Constance and took her arm. Constance looked around, but Countess Christina Anderson was already absorbed in her own private conversation with Sir Hightower. Sir Ralph appeared to be extremely intelligent and very subtle in his conversation. Constance felt very uneasy with this young man.

"What brings you to Bellingfast?" Sir Adams asked.

"My aunt, my cousin, and I had planned this vacation several months ago," she answered.

"Who is your aunt, and who is your cousin?" Sir Ralph Adams inquired.

He was very insistent for an answer. Constance was very skeptical, and she flat out did not want to give him any information about herself or her family members.

"Oh!" she exclaimed. "Here comes Sir Hightower."

She abruptly left Sir Ralph Adams and took Sir Hightower's arm. "Why don't we play the rest of the tournament by ourselves?"

"Well, okay," he replied. They walked together toward the empty tennis court.

The barns and horse stables made up a unique complex located in a perfect place. The trails from the barn went into the forest and the mountains that surrounded the estate. All the country trails were perfect for horseback riders. The barn complex consisted of two buildings. One building held all the equipment, and the other building housed the twenty-five thoroughbreds.

William Jeffery Toler was the riding instructor. He was a young man and quite well-trained to manage the Bellingfast stables. He was a true southern gentleman. Lady Lindsey and his father attended the same prestigious finishing academy in New Hampshire in America. Jeffery came highly recommended by Lady Lindsey when he applied to work at Bellingfast Estates. He had majored in veterinary science and minored in European anthropology. He became an invaluable asset in Madam MaRooska's international business. He had broad shoulders and a sheepish grin. All the young ladies who visited the estate wanted to have special riding lessons with the carefree equestrian. William Jeffery managed the entire estate and riding arena with the assistance of ten stable boys.

Madam MaRooska provided Jeffery with a plush apartment complex on the estate grounds. Jeffery spent most of his time at the riding academy, but Madam MaRooska had also provided Jeffery with a nice little flat in town. It was a genuinely nice arrangement for a young man, but it was a very demanding and extremely dangerous career.

Chapter 5

Stormy Trail Ride and Lady Lindsey Disappears

"Well, Sir Hightower," Jeffery said. "I got your message, and I have both of the horses ready for your afternoon ride."

"That's great," Sir Hightower responded.

"Miss Stallings will be riding Windy Tide, and you, sir, will be riding Lord of All-Seattle Slew. Both are remarkable thoroughbreds. I am sure both of you will enjoy the afternoon." Jeffery paused and then said, "Oh, by the way, Countess Christina was also in after lunch. She told me that you had invited her and Sir Ralph Adams to join you on the ride."

Sir Hightower looked puzzled. "Well, I really do not remember saying that, but we did play tennis with them this morning. Maybe it just slipped my mind."

“Maybe so,” Jeffery agreed. “Well, I must be getting back to work. Countess Christina said you all would be leaving around four.”

Sir Hightower walked back to the estate, still wondering how the countess knew so much about the plans for the afternoon ride. Meanwhile, back up in room 202, Constance was talking with Lady Lindsey about the day’s activities.

“So, you did not enjoy the day with Sir Hightower?” Lady Lindsey asked.

Constance hesitated a minute, and then she said, “We were not alone. One of those Barbados twins was on the tennis court, and he insisted that Sir Hightower and I play doubles with them. We never got away from Ralph Adams.”

“How exciting,” Virginia Camille commented. “Is he as interesting as he appears to be?”

“I don’t know. He is very nosy. He was asking all about you and Lady Lindsey.”

“Well, I guess I must have intrigued him at the masquerade ball,” Virginia Camille said, beaming with enthusiasm.

“I guess so, Virginia Camille, but I did not tell him one detail about us. I hope Sir Hightower and I enjoy each other’s company while riding the trails this afternoon.”

“I hope so too,” Lady Lindsey admitted. “He is such a nice man.”

“How nice, how nice,” Virginia Camille sarcastically remarked. “I’ll think of you when I’m in the library, playing chess, with old stuffed shirt."

"Please be nice," Lady Lindsey advised Virginia again. "Do not set the stage for a bad reputation. And you can do that. You can do just that!"

The phone rang, and Constance answered. It was Sir Hightower inquiring after her. "Yes, I'm ready." Then she turned to Lady Lindsey. "I really did not expect him until after 5:00 PM, but I am ready."

"Have a nice time, dear," Lady Lindsey remarked.

Both girls went down the stairs at the same time. Constance was going to meet Sir Hightower, and Virginia Camille was making her way toward the library. William Jeffery was in his plush apartment complex on the grounds. He was watching a video. The screen showed one of his star students as she was preparing for competition, which was to be held at Londonberry Estates. Londonberry Estates were owned by Lord Tutwiller. The competition was to begin in two weeks, and Jeffery wanted to be sure his contestant was prepared.

When the phone rang, Jeffery answered, saying, "Jeffery here. You do? When? You had not mentioned that. I will be in the stable in ten minutes."

Jeffery turned the video off, put on his shirt, jumped into his Jeep, and drove to the stables. As he got near the barn, he could tell that Constance was terribly upset.

When he got out of the Jeep, Constance ran into his arms. "Jeffery, Jeffery, I'm so scared! I'm afraid it's going to happen all over again!"

Jeffery tried to quite her down, but Constance was almost uncontrollable. "Just tell me what has happened."

Constance was crying hysterically.

Sir Hightower began to explain. "I do not know what is wrong. I know Constance was not expecting to see Sir Ralph Adams or the countess, but I never expected her to react in this way. He told her that Ralph and the countess were going to ride with them up into the forest trails. Ralph whispered something into her ear, and she went hysterical. I could not quiet her down. That's when I had her to call you."

"Constance, Constance calm down," Jeffery ordered her.

Jeffery abruptly turned to question Ralph. "What did you say to her?"

Ralph acted as though he had not said much of importance at all. "Let us quit procrastinating. I am ready to go for our horseback ride. I've been planning this outing all afternoon. Come on, countess, let's start the trail ride."

The stable boys helped Ralph and the countess onto their horses, and they started the trail ride toward the forest and mountains. Sir Hightower was still trying to console Constance. Sir Hightower knew nothing about Constance's previous visit or about her book.

As Virginia Camille stepped into the library, Charles moved toward the door to meet her. Virginia smiled to Charles, but she was very satisfied because she knew this would be her last evening with him. It did not matter that he and she had been paired together. Virginia knew this would be their last time together. That fact made her incredibly happy.

"I've already got us a special place picked out," Charles announced.

Then he escorted her to a private little table in the corner of the room. He helped her sit down, and she sat on the other side of the table. The ivory antique chess set had already been set up for the two chess players. Virginia Camille inquisitively gazed about the room to see what all was going on. There were four persons seated at one of the tables near them. Virginia Camille had met Sir Reggie Adams at the masquerade ball, but she did not know the other three persons seated with him.

"Charles," Virginia began. "Who are the people playing bridge?"

Promptly, Doctor Charles Wellington began to give her information about the guests at the table. "The older lady with red hair is Doctor Harriot Ashbury. She is the governor of Arizona from the United States. Her bridge partner is Elwood Harper. He is an Australian stockbroker. He is quite a nice gentleman. I talked with him extensively at the masquerade ball."

"I recognize Sir Reggie Adams," Virginia Camille said. "But who is his bridge partner?"

"Her name is Lelia Alessia Rameno," Charles answered. "She is from Italy, a business executive from San Marita. I have talked with her, but I do not know much about her. She seems rather distant."

A beautiful young lady walked across the room. She whispered something into a man's ear, and he abruptly left the room and followed her out the door and down the corridor.

"What was that all about?" Virginia Camille asked.

"I have no idea," he admitted. "But are you ready for our game of chess? I'm ready to give you the game of your life."

At that, they started their chess match.

Several hours went by, and the library began to fill up with other guests. The library was the one room that best reflected intellect and personality. The invited guests always enjoyed spending time in the library. Many of the guests got so involved with reading that they would check out books and read before retiring to bed.

There was a black marble fireplace with walnut paneling over mantle. British and French tapestries hung all around the room. The ceiling was painted by a French artist. Virginia Camille looked toward the door. She was quite surprised to see Lady Lindsey, Madam MaRooska, and Lord Tutwiller coming through the library entrance.

"Excuse me," Virginia Camille said. "I didn't realize Lady Lindsey was going to be out tonight. I must go speak with her."

Sir Wellington stood up, and Virginia Camille approached the three of them. "Lady Lindsey, so surprised to see you. You mentioned nothing to me about being out tonight."

Lord Tutwiller put his arm around Lady Lindsey. "I couldn't resist seeing her again," he said, bragging, "She has made quite an impression on me."

"She makes quite an impression on each person she comes in contact with," Madam MaRooska said.

"I totally agree," he said. Lord Tutwiller put his arm through hers and continued, "I would like to show you some of our mystery novels."

The two of them walked toward the library cases. There was a William and Mary grandfather clock standing in the corner of the room. It had a flat-roofed head and a cornice supported on a twisted column.

The signature read: Daniel Quale, London.

As Lord Tutwiller began to speak, a secret peephole on the face of the clock opened. The revolving eye scanned the room and focused on Lord Tutwiller and Lady Lindsey.

"Would you like to join us?" Virginia Camille asked. "Doctor Wellington and I are enjoying a game of chess."

Then the two of them walked back toward the corner of the room. When Doctor Wellington saw Madam MaRooska coming, he pulled up another chair.

"Are you enjoying yourself, Doctor Wellington?" Madam MaRooska asked.

"Positively remarkable," he agreed. "You couldn't have matched me up any better. I am delighted with Virginia Camille. She is so interesting and witty. I hope she feels the same about me."

Virginia Camille just smiled and winked at Doctor Wellington, but it did not mean a thing, not one thing!

As the people in the library looked out the windows, the skies began to darken. The winds began to blow and whirl about. Several of the guests began to feel a little uneasy as the thunder and lightning began to roar. The skies got darker and darker.

Sir Callahan had been sent up to the library. "Madam MaRooska, the weather is looking bad. James has instructed us to turn the intercom off on the bottom floor. We have enough generators if the electricity goes off."

"That's a good idea," Madam MaRooska remarked. "I'll be down in a minute."

As Sir Callahan was leaving the library, William Jeffery rushed toward Madam MaRooska.

He said, "Madam MaRooska, I am very worried. The riding party left this afternoon around 4:00 PM. There were no signs of bad weather at that time, but this dreadful weather has taken over, and the riding party has not returned."

"What trails did they take?" Madam MaRooska asked.

"They took the Lake Forest trail, and the Mountain Brook view beside the old cave."

"That can be a dangerous ride," Madam MaRooska said, explaining, "Especially if the weather is bad."

As they looked out the window, the rain was coming down in sheets, and the leaves were whirling around. Branches were everywhere.

"We had best send somebody out to look them," Madam MaRooska advised.

"I'll gather up a couple of boys, and we'll start to scout toward the trails," William Jeffery assured her.

The guests began to stand up. Some of the guests walked over to one of the large picture windows to see what was happening outside. All at once, a loud sound like a screech and a loud crack were heard. Immediately following that, all the lights went out, and it was totally dark.

"Relax," Madam MaRooska said. "Just relax. I sent word, and we will have candles shortly."

Five minutes had passed, and Madam MaRooska made another appeal. "Just stay seated. Sir Callahan and Sir Richardson are on their way to get the candelabras for light. The glow from the candelabras will shed enough light for you to see your way around."

All the guests were excited. They were all talking at once. Everyone was confused, trying to figure out just what had happened. Then, just as mysteriously as the lights went out, they miraculously came back on. The guests were quite relieved. Many guests had decided that they had had enough for one night, and most decided to retire to their own rooms.

As the guests looked around, Virginia Camille became frightened. She was looking around for Lady Lindsey, and she was nowhere to be found.

"Stop!" Constance hollered. "Where is Lady Lindsey? Where is my aunt?"

All the guests began to search for the missing elderly Lady Lindsey Stallings.

Lord Tutwiller was especially concerned. "When the lights went out, I was holding her arm. Then she must have slipped away. I fumbled around in the dark. I called her name. I figured she must have wandered across the room. When Madam MaRooska assured everyone that the candles were on the way, I did not worry anymore. But now it's obvious that she is not here."

"Do not be alarmed," said Madam MaRooska. "I am sure she is alright. She is probably in her room."

"Well, I'm going to look for her myself," said Virginia Camille.

She left the room with Doctor Wellington close behind. Camille quickly raced out of the library and ran up the winding staircase. When she got upstairs, she went through her room and into Lady Lindsey's room.

"Just as I figured," Virginia Camille said. "She is not here."

Looking around her room, Virginia Camille was puzzled. There was a black package wrapped in a red bow on the bed. Virginia Camille did not hesitate one moment. She opened the package. Inside the package was the angel doll. Virginia Camille screamed, and then she fainted. She had been standing next to the bed, and when she passed out, she was literally draped over it.

From the closet next to the window, a figure approached. The figure grabbed the black package and removed the contents. The figure then replaced the contents with a red rose. Immediately, the figure disappeared out the window. Virginia Camille had fainted due to the stress and the commotion of the last hour.

Earlier, Doctor Wellington had followed Virginia Camille when she had abruptly left the library in search of her aunt. By the time Doctor Wellington got to Virginia Camille, she had fainted and was draped over the bed. Doctor Wellington came right in to investigate what was going on. Virginia Camille was dumbfounded, and she could not say a word.

Doctor Wellington called the front desk. "Please send a doctor to room 201 – I mean, room 202. I will be waiting for the doctor. I am Doctor Wellington."

Moments later, the house doctor arrived. "I'm Doctor Fitzgerald. I'm on call tonight."

When he went over to her, Virginia Camille was lying on the bed with the black package next to her body.

"What has happened?" the doctor asked.

"I really don't know," Doctor Wellington said. "We were in the library, and the lights went out. Virginia ran out looking for her aunt. She was hysterical."

The doctor began to check her pulse. Then he checked her heart. "Seems as though she fainted. Her vital signs are all intact. Here, let us prop her up on the pillow. It will be easier on her when she awakens."

Several moments went by, and then Virginia Camille slowly opened her eyes. "What happened? What happened?" she asked.

Madam MaRooska, Lord Tutwiller, and Lady Lindsey walked into the room. Virginia Camille still could not talk. She blinked her eyes several times, but she could not say a word.

"A lot of strange events have taken place tonight," Lord Tutwiller remarked.

Agreeing with him, Lady Lindsey tried to assure Virginia Camille that she was safe.

Then Dr. Wellington inquired, "Where did you go, Lady Lindsey?"

"I will tell you later, but first we must be sure Virginia Camille is alright."

As she looked around the room, Lady Lindsey spied the black package on her bed and looked inside. "Oh... a beautiful red rose. Wonder who it is from?"

"Is there a card?" Madam MaRooska inquired. "Yes, it says it's from an admirer."

"How pretty," Lady Lindsey said. "We'll need to put it in a vase."

Then Lord Tutwiller announced, "Madam MaRooska, the weather has cleared up somewhat. Have James bring the limo around, and I will return to Londonberry." He then kissed Lady Lindsey on her cheek and suggested they have lunch the next day.

"That sounds wonderful, providing Virginia Camille is alright," Lady Lindsey said. "I'll see you tomorrow."

Lord Tutwiller left. The jumped into the limo out front and began his journey back to Londonberry Estates.

Madam MaRooska was still chatting with Doctor Fitzgerald. "Is she okay, doctor?"

"Yes, she will be fine," he said. "Just let her rest. I guess all the excitement must have exhausted her. However, you might suggest that she does not do any strenuous activities tomorrow. Rest a day or so before continuing the daily planned activities."

Madam MaRooska realized that Doctor Wellington was still concerned about Lady Lindsey's disappearance.

Lady Lindsey tried to make Virginia Camille as comfortable as she could. She pulled back the covers on the bed as Virginia got under them.

Thirty minutes passed. There was a knock at the door. It was Madam MaRooska.

"Lady Lindsey, I hate to tell you this."

"Tell me what?"

"Constance is missing," she explained.

"What are you talking about?" Lady Lindsey was shocked and very much disturbed.

"A party of four left the estate this afternoon at 4:00 PM, and they have not returned. William Jeffery approached me around 6:30. He was alarmed. He and two stable hands immediately started the search. However, it was to no avail.

"Did they look everywhere?" Lady Lindsey asked calmly.

Madam MaRooska was somewhat alarmed and responded, "William Jeffery and the boys followed the Lake Forest trail, and then went on to the mountain view. There was no sign of the riders. I feel sure the trail riders must have detoured, as the storm got worse. I knew there were heavy winds and hail."

"Why, Madam MaRooska, did they go horseback riding on such a dangerous night?" Lady Lindsey asked.

"No bad weather was forecasted," Madam MaRooska assured her. "We would have never let them leave Bellingfast. Severe weather and abrupt thunderstorms are prevalent in these parts, but I assure you that, at the time of departure, the weather was permissible."

Lady Lindsey remembered what Major Devonshire and Colonel Beacham had warned them about before they left Parkview Plantation. Lady Lindsey was beginning to wish she had taken the men more seriously.

Perhaps, Lady Lindsey thought, this is not a safe place to be. After all, we have only been here two days, and strange incidents have already begun to occur.

As Madam MaRooska left the room, she said, "I'm going on back. When I hear anything, I'll contact you."

"Thanks," Lady Lindsey said fretfully. "Please do keep me informed."

Glancing around her room, Lady Lindsey noticed that Virginia Camille was beginning to arouse. Lady Lindsey went over to her and tried to give her a glass of water. Virginia sat up in the bed. She was fully awake by now.

"Lady Lindsey...Lady Lindsey. What is going on here?" Virginia Camille stammered.

"Darling, believe me, I do not know," Lady Lindsey tried to explain.

"What is going on?" Virginia Camille knew something was terribly wrong.

"Virginia, I need to tell you, first things first...Constance is missing."

"What?!" she screamed. Virginia sat up in the bed and was dumbfounded. "I knew she and Sir Hightower were going horseback riding."

"Well, they never returned," Lady Lindsey admitted.

Virginia Camille looked at her watch. It was well after midnight. "So, where are they?"

"Madam MaRooska assumes that when the treacherous storm blew up, the riders took a detour to find shelter."

Virginia Camille got up and went to the window. She looked out at the storm. The winds were still howling. Blowing rain and hail were hitting the windowpanes, and the shutters were blowing back and forth.

Virginia Camille moaned. "I am worried. I am so worried."

"So am I," Lady Lindsey agreed with her. "So am I."

Constance did not enjoy the trail ride. First, she did not like the twins from Barbados. She had gathered enough information from Lord Tutwiller that she was very skeptical of their purpose for coming to the event at Bellingfast Estates. She really did not want to have anything to do with these young men, and now she was on a trail ride with Sir Ralph Grantly Adams III.

Sir Hightower tried his best to ease Constance's worries. "Constance, try to relax. This ride can be very calming. Just look at the pretty scenery. This forest trail ride provides a spectacular view with the wildflowers and the tall Scots pine trees."

Constance finally began to relax. Yes, the view was magnificent, and the woodland trail was calming. Constance knew the twins were dangerous men. However, she tried to block out the inappropriate comments and gestures that were made by them at the stables. She gazed at Sir Hightower, smiled, and thought, Yes, I do believe he is a nice and sincere gentleman. I do hope to get to know him better during the visit at Bellingfast.

"Sir Hightower," Constance said. "You have made mention that you are an author."

"Yes, Constance, I have had numerous books published and several series of poems added to my collection of writings."

"What is your specialty?"

"I love writing mystery novels," he answered. "But I

do dabble in British politics."

"How unique."

"I hear you are a writer," Sir Hightower interjected. He was trying to get more information about Constance.

"Why do you say that?" Constance interjected.

"Sir Ralph told me when we were on the tennis court."

"Oh..."

Constance was shocked.

She had not told anyone about her last visit to Bellingfast, and she certainly had not shared anything about the tragedy or the death of the lady who had stolen the angel doll. She just wanted to forget the last visit, so she could finish the last chapters of her book. Then she could send it to the publisher. Constance did not say another word about her writing. She just continued to ride on, pretending she did not hear the last question. But that comment from Sir Hightower confirmed her belief that those Barbados twins were bad news. Constance knew they were up to something, but she could not pinpoint anything at this time.

As they rode on through the forest, the winds began to pick up and blow and whirl in all directions.

"Looks like we are heading into a rainstorm," Sir Hightower acknowledged.

"I hope it blows over soon," Constance stammered. "I'm getting frightened."

Several minutes later, Sir Ralph Adams and the countess were heading back toward them.

"The storm is bad!" The countess shrieked. "We had to turn around."

"The storm has torn up tree trunks and scattered loose branches all over the trail," Sir Ralph explained. "The rain is coming down so hard that you can't even see two feet ahead of you."

"The fog is getting heavy," Sir Hightower noted. "If we do not find a place soon, I don't know if we can make it through the night."

"Follow me," Sir Ralph said. "I saw a small wooded cove leading into a cave near the mountain view. I think we can make it if we hurry."

Thunder and lightning lit up the sky. Hail began to come down, and wind currents continued to whirl in all directions. The horses were frightened. They did not like this weather either. Branches and shrubbery were flying everywhere. After a tumultuous escape out of the forest, the trail riders found themselves safe in the small cove outside a mountain cliff. They were relieved and thankful that their lives had been spared.

Sir Hightower and Sir Ralph had to get the horses secured and in a safe place. Rains and winds were still coming down, and the thunder was still sounding in the skies overhead.

"Constance, why don't we go on in closer to the opening of the cave?" Countess Christina suggested. "I think it will be somewhat safer for us." Constance followed her deeper into the cave.

"I hear you are a writer," said the countess.

"Well, I haven't broadcasted it while on my trip. How did you know? "Constance asked.

"Oh, Sir Ralph told me," The Countess replied. "He

knows a lot about each guest here at Bellingfast, and what he doesn't know, he and his brother will find out before the two weeks is up."

"How interesting," is all that Constance could say.

With the rustling of bushes and branches, in walked Sir Hightower and Ralph Adams.

"We got the horses settled," Sir Hightower said. "But I'm afraid we will be here all night."

"Oh, no," Constance sighed. "Are you sure we cannot make it out later on?"

"The fog is so bad," Sir Ralph explained. "Besides, that lightning and thunder have not let up, and the rain is still pouring down."

"It would simply be too dangerous to get back on the trails until daybreak!" Sir Hightower exclaimed.

"So..." Constance said. "What do we do now?"

"Let's look around the cave for a warm and safe spot to lie down and perhaps get some sleep," the countess suggested.

"Where are we, anyway?" Constance asked.

"We are at the base of the cliffs of Moher," the countess replied. "When you climb to the top, you can see the magic and mystery and magnificent views from the cliffs of Moher."

"The cliffs of Moher are the most iconic features in Ireland's landscape," Sir Hightower added. "The cliffs stretch eight kilometers along the Atlantic coastline. This is Ireland's most visited natural attraction. Over one million people come to experience the cliffs each year. Moher, when translated, means 'the ruined fort'.

Nothing remains of the fort. Moher Tower is still in place today."

"There is another important tower," said Sir Ralph. "It is called O'Brien's Tower. This man was a local landowner, and he believed that if they developed tourism in this area it would help the people out of poverty and help the economy."

"Did we bring anything to eat?" Constance asked.

"Yes," Sir Ralph answered. "Inside each saddle bag, William Jeffery provided a small snack, water, crackers, cheese, chips, and wafer bread. So, when we decide to eat, we do have something to nibble on until morning."

"Good," The countess replied. "We'll need it."

Constance began to worry. "I know the people back at Bellingfast are concerned about us."

"No use trying to make contact with your cell phones," Sir Hightower reminded them. "We have no service this far out. Besides, I don't know if we could get in with this bad weather."

"So, we are just stuck 'til morning?" Constance complained.

Sir Hightower eased close to Constance and tried to comfort her, saying, "It won't be too bad."

It seemed Sir Hightower was looking forward to being with Constance all night.

"I brought a blanket from my home," Sir Hightower encouraged her. "Come on, Constance. Let us find a nice comfortable spot and try to settle down for the night."

Sir Hightower put his strong arm around Constance and encouraged her to lay her head on his chest. He knew she had had an exhausting day. He found a secluded spot in the cave. He laid the blanket down and Constance shared the warmth of the blanket. Sir Hightower was very much beginning to feel something for Constance. As they lay on the blanket, he kissed her several times. Her sweet lips were so soft. Thirty minutes passed, and Sir Hightower was wide awake. Constance had already gone to sleep.

Back in another part of the cave, Sir Ralph and the countess were engaged in a stimulating conversation. They were both sitting on the blanket that Sir Ralph had brought. They were enjoying the snacks that Sir Jeffery had sent.

"So, when will your divorce be finalized?" Sir Ralph intuitively quizzed the countess.

Stunned by his question, the countess replied, "What makes you think I am getting a divorce?"

"You haven't lived in Stirling Castle for over eight months, and the earl spends the majority of his time in London," Sir Ralph explained.

"Just because we've not been together, it does not necessarily mean divorce," the countess quickly clarified.

"You are so right, but how does it add up that you stay at the Spencer summer residence half the year?" Sir Ralph quizzed again.

"Edmund Spencer is my business advisor and confidant. My husband is aware of the time I am spending at the Spencer summer house, and he totally approves. Do you have any more questions, Sir Ralph Adams? Any more questions?"

“Not currently, countess, not at this time. But I am sure I will have more questions in time,” Sir Ralph assured her. The countess and Sir Ralph each got on their own blanket and slept until daybreak.

As the sun was beginning to find its way over the horizon, there was a rustling and cracking of branches in the bushes outside the cave.

“There are the horses!” a stable boy exclaimed.

“Yes!” the other boy cried. “I hope they are safe. I hope they made it through the night.”

When William Jeffery finally made it to the cave, he was very relieved. The storm the night before was a very treacherous one, and everyone at Bellingfast was worried about the trail riders’ safety.

As William Jeffery made his way through the tangled brush and bushes, he hollered, “Are you safe?”

Startled, the four trail riders began to wake up.

“Yes, yes, William Jeffery!” Constance cried. “We are in here.”

As William Jeffery made his way into the cave, he saw that the four people were all safe. The cave had provided a safe shelter while the storm was going on. Constance was the first to get up. She ran to William Jeffery and hugged him. Then she began to cry.

“It’s okay, Constance,” William Jeffery consoled her. “It’s okay.”

Then Sir Hightower approached Constance. He put his arm around her. He kissed her on the cheek. He had picked up the blanket on which they had slept. The two of them headed outside to their horses.

"Are you all alright?" William Jeffery asked Sir Ralph.

"As well as can be expected, you might say," said Sir Ralph. He then picked up his blanket and went out of the cave and got on his horse.

"Countess, countess!" William Jeffery said, and then he apologized for Sir Ralph's rudeness. "Let me help you."

"Thank you, William Jeffery," the countess said, assuring him, "It has been a stressful night, but I am okay."

William Jeffery helped the countess out of the cave, and she rode next to William Jeffery back to Bellingfast.

Back in room 201 at Bellingfast Estates, Constance finally made her way to her family. She walked through to the connecting room to find Lady Lindsey seated at her desk. Virginia Camille had just awakened from her sleep. The doctor had given her a sedative. She had quite an ordeal from the preceding night. When Lady Lindsey saw Constance, she immediately got up and ran toward her.

Lady Lindsey was incredibly happy and relieved to see Constance. "I've been up all night worrying about you," she admitted. "Come lay down on the bed while I order you some breakfast."

Virginia Camille aroused from her sleep. When she saw Constance, she was ecstatic and hysterical. "What happened?" she exclaimed. "What happened to you all?"

Constance tried to explain everything as best she could. "While we were on the trail ride, that horrendous storm blew in. The weather was so bad. The limbs and branches were flying everywhere, and the fog was so thick that you could not see two feet ahead. The horses were in a panic. So, we located a cave at the base of the cliffs of Moher. We spent the night there."

There was a knock at the door. Lady Lindsey opened it to find Sir Callahan bringing in two trays with breakfast.

"I knew Virginia Camille was quite upset from last night, so I brought her a breakfast tray along with one for Constance," Sir Callahan said.

"Thank you, Sir Callahan," Lady Lindsey said, acknowledged him.

Sir Callahan left the room, and Lady Lindsey got the two girls situated so they could eat their breakfast.

"Don't talk, girls," Lady Lindsey suggested. "Just try to eat this nourishing food. You both need it."

After the girls had finished their breakfast, Lady Lindsey said, "Girls, we have a lot to talk about. A lot has happened in the last twenty-four hours."

Virginia Camille put her hand over her ears. "I do not understand, I do not understand what all went on last night. I want an explanation. Where did you go after the light went out, Lady Lindsey? Where did you go?"

"Well, darling..." Lady Lindsey began to try to explain. "I really do not know. When the light went out, I was standing with Lord Tutwiller. He was showing me all the mystery novels that Madam MaRooska had collected over the years. Many of the writers, poets, and authors had spent time at Bellingfast Estates. When the lights went out, I was shoved behind the mantle and blindfolded. Then I was forced to go to the elevator."

"Who was talking to you and telling you what to do?" Virginia Camille inquired.

"Not a word was spoken. Someone pushed me every step of the way. Somebody embraced me so I would not fall, but not a word was whispered," Lady Lindsey explained.

"So, what happened next?" Virginia Camille asked.

"Well, when the elevator stopped, I was pushed out. The elevator closed, and I guess it went back up to the upper levels. I was left alone, so I took off my blindfold. I must have been in the boiler room. There were pipes and heavy equipment all over the room. There were several dim lights on in the room, so I could see. I followed a tiny hallway into another room, which must have been the cellar. There were rows and rows of shelves of aged wines. This room was well lighted, so I knew where I was. There was a door. I tried to get out, but it must have been locked. I banged and beat on the door. Then about fifteen minutes or more lapsed. Sir Richardson opened the cellar door. I told him I could not get out. I do not know how I even got here."

"We have a revolving mantle in the library," Sir Richardson explained. "You must have stood on the button that opens the door. The elevator took you down two floors."

"But why couldn't I open the door?" I asked him.

"The cellar door is broken. The latch has not been repaired, so I had to use a key to open the door. Let me escort you to the garden hall, and you can make your way on up to your room."

Lady Lindsey continued with her story. "As I was walking through the main hall, I was met by Madam MaRooska and Lord Tutwiller. Madam MaRooska told me Virginia Camille had taken sick and that the house doctor, Doctor Charles Fitzgerald, was with her. And that is all I really know about last night."

Virginia Camille began to quiz her. "What happened to your angel doll?"

"Well, I thought you knew," Constance answered. "I put the doll back in the family vault at Parkview Plantation."

"Have you opened the vault since you put the doll in there three years ago?" Virginia Camille asked demandingly.

"No," Constance replied. "There was no use to open the vault or even look for the doll. I assure you she was locked up safely in the family vault."

Virginia Camille began to describe the horrible experience when she had opened the black package. "Your angel doll was inside the black package."

"You must have been mistaken," Constance explained. "You must have been so upset that you saw wrong."

"Yes, dear," Lady Lindsey added. "When I looked in the package, it was a red rose. We put the red rose in a vase. You must have been very disoriented when I disappeared."

"I may have been disoriented and delusional, but believe me I recognized that angel doll. Constance and I played with that doll our entire childhoods, and I certainly recognized her. But I do not know how she disappeared before you got back into the room. Somebody must have taken the doll and swapped the doll with a rose."

"But nobody knew about the doll!" Lady Lindsey exclaimed.

"Oh, yes, they did," Constance said. "Those Barbados twins must know everything about us. When we were on the trail ride, the countess shared with me that those boys from Barbados knew everything about all of the guests here at Bellingfast Estates."

"The countess could be wrong, couldn't she?" Lady Lindsey argued.

"I believe her," Constance muttered.

"Why, dear, why?" Lady Lindsey questioned her.

"Because, when we started the trail ride..." Constance began to explain. "Sir Ralph Grantly Adams whispered in my ear."

"Whispered what?!" Virginia Camille screamed.

Constance continued, saying, "He asked me if I brought my angel doll this trip. I had not told a soul about my visit three years ago to Bellingfast, and I am sure he knew the entire story about the murder at Londonberry Estates."

"Yes! Yes!" Virginia Camille shrieked. "It was the angel doll. I am sure the angel doll was in the black package."

"Girls, girls," Lady Lindsey began, trying to reassure them. "We cannot say another word to anyone about this. I am not going to say anything to Madam MaRooska, and promise me you girls will remain silent regarding this matter. We will figure out what to do and how this will affect all of us. Do not say a word to anyone."

Constance and Virginia Camille went through the connecting doors and back into their room. Constance had to bathe. After that, she planned to take a nap. She had missed so much sleep the night before. Virginia Camille was still very puzzled about everything that had happened the night before. She knew beyond a shadow of a doubt that the angel doll was somewhere in Bellingfast Estates. How the doll got there or why the doll was there or who put the doll in the black sack were all still part of this mystery. It was a big mystery, but Virginia Camille was going to solve it herself. She was going to start by talking to Sir Ralph Grantly Adams the first chance she got.

The phone rang, and Lady Lindsey answered. "Hello? Oh, yes, much better. I'll see you at 11:30."

Then Lady Lindsey went through the connecting doors to room 202. Constance was already asleep, and Virginia Camille was getting dressed.

"Virginia, dear," Lady Lindsey addressed her. "I'll be leaving shortly. Lord Tutwiller is taking me out to Londonberry Estates. You realize that the three races are scheduled for next week, yes?"

"Oh, yes, I remember," Virginia Camille responded. "This horse show is Ireland's peak social and sporting event."

"Yes, it is," Lady Lindsey said. "And visitors and contestants from across the globe will be there for the festivities. Lord Tutwiller hosts the event every year, and I'm so glad we'll be able to attend." She was incredibly proud.

"I'm glad, too, Lady Lindsey. I am too." Virginia Camille said. "You run along and give my love to Lord Tutwiller. I've got a million things to do today."

As Lady Lindsey was leaving, she reminded Virginia Camille, "Do not forget, Doctor Fitzgerald suggested that you take it easy today. Do not get over exhausted."

Lady Lindsey walked to the door, and Virginia Camille reassured her, "Oh, I won't. I'll take it slow and easy."

"Good," Lady Lindsey remarked.

Lady Lindsey was satisfied with Virginia Camille's response but really wondered if she would do what she said she would do.

Virginia Camille quietly tiptoed over to Constance. Constance was sound asleep. Virginia decided to mosey down to the library.

She entered the library and sighed to herself, Great! Nobody is in here.

Then she glanced toward the corner of the room, and she saw Elizabeth Ann and Reuben. They were sitting in high-backed leather wing chairs. They seemed to be reading.

How inconvenient, she thought.

Walking toward the two, she said, "Good morning."

Elizabeth Ann was quick to respond. "Good morning to you, Virginia Camille, and how did you sleep last night in this treacherous storm?"

"Well, I managed to sleep, but I was so worried about Constance."

"Yes," Rueben interrupted. "We heard that the riding party spent the night in a cave outside of the cliffs of Moher."

"Is Constance all right?" Elizabeth Ann questioned.

"Yes," Virginia Camille answered. "But I do believe she and the party will do a lot of sleeping today to catch up with the sleep they lost last night."

"I suppose so," Reuben said. He then looked at his watch and said, "Virginia Camille, you must excuse us. We haven't eaten breakfast, and Elizabeth Ann suggested we go to the main dining hall for brunch."

"Would you like to join us?" Elizabeth Ann asked.

"No, I had planned to check out some books that Lord Tutwiller suggested. Several authors have donated books to Madam MaRooska's library, and Lord Tutwiller highly recommended them."

Then Rueben stood up and helped Elizabeth Ann up, and they proceeded to the main dining hall for brunch.

Chapter 6

Virginia Camille Investigates

When they were out of the room, Virginia Camille briskly walked over to the fireplace. She cautiously gazed around the room to be sure she was alone. As she approached the mantle, she keenly observed the flooring around the mantle. She spied an elevated button about the size of a fifty-cent piece. When she stepped on the button, a small passage behind the mantle revolved around. When Virginia Camille stepped inside the passageway, the door immediately closed, and the mantle move back into its place. She was in a small elevator, and it was going down, just as Lady Lindsey had said. When the elevator door opened the second time, Virginia Camille stepped out. As Lady Lindsey reported, this must have been the boiler room.

Virginia Camille decided to look around for herself. She was going to be quite observant of anything that looked suspicious. As she was rummaging around the heavy equipment, steel pipes, and cardboard boxes, her leg brushed up against an aluminum crate. She noticed that the leg of her pants had accumulated some blood stains. She bent down and pulled out the small aluminum crate. As she opened the aluminum crate, she saw a bloody glove. The glove was wrapped around something. Peering into the crate, Virginia Camille knew her suspicions were correct. Somebody had done something illegal or wrong because the angel doll was hidden in the aluminum crate and wrapped in the bloody glove. But where did the blood come from? And who put it there? And better yet—why was the angel doll back in the picture?

Virginia Camille shoved the aluminum crate back on the shelf. Remembering what Lady Lindsey had reported, she went through a tiny hallway, which led to the wine cellar. However, this time, she was able to open the door. Looking at the latch from the outside, it was obvious that the latch had been broken. Someone wanted Lady Lindsey to be in the wine cellar for a certain amount of time. Then when the time was up, they allowed Lady Lindsey to come out. Virginia walked out of the cellar and went through to the main hall. She knew she was not going to say a word to anyone. However, she still intended to quiz Sir Ralph Grantly Adams. Hopefully, this mystery would unravel.

Virginia Camille just kept remembering those words.

These boys from Barbados are dangerous.

Just how much danger was involved would be determined later.

Chapter 7

Tour of Londonberry Estates

When Lord Tutwiller entered the building, he immediately went to the garden hall. He figured, if Lady Lindsey was not present, he would have to have Sir Richardson or Sir Callahan page her to come down. However, as he started toward the information desk, he heard his name called.

"Lord Tutwiller, Lord Tutwiller!" Lady Lindsey called. "Come over here."

As he approached the ladies, he noticed that Lady Lindsey was seated with a middle- aged lady whom he did not recognize.

"Good morning, ladies," he said, addressing the wom- en.

"Lord Tutwiller," Lady Lindsey asked. "Do you know Miss Romano?"

"Please, Lord Tutwiller, just call me Lelia Allesia," she responded.

"Lelia Allesia, it is. So nice to meet you." He shook her hand. "Lady Lindsey and I are going to drive out to Londonberry Estates. Would you like to go with us?"

"I'd like to, but I am waiting on Sir Reggie Renaldo."

"He's one of those twins from Barbados, is he not?" Lord Tutwiller wanted clarification.

"Yes, I met him at the masquerade ball. We were paired together. I have enjoyed his company. He and his brother seem so nice."

Lord Tutwiller raised his eyebrows with displeasure as he concentrated his thoughts on the information he had been given about the Barbados twins.

"Do I see disapproval on you face?" Lelia Allesia asked.

"No," Lord Tutwiller quickly answered. "I was thinking about something else." Then he abruptly took Lady Lindsey by the elbow and said, "We need to be going. So nice to meet you, and your name is what again?"

"Lelia Allesia Romano," she responded.

"And where did you say you are from?"

Lady Lindsey answered for her. "Italy. She is from San Marino, Italy."

As the limo was traveling from Bellingfast to Londonberry, Ireland, Lord Tutwiller was becoming more and more excited about the upcoming horse racing events.

"Is this the first time you have been to a horse racing event?" Lord Tutwiller asked.

"Yes, it is," Lady Lindsey replied. "Several of my family members have been to the Kentucky Derby in the states, but this is the first event for me."

"This will be a two-day festival. Ten to twenty thousand people will attend the festival."

"Where do they all stay?" Lady Lindsey asked.

"I can accommodate seventy-five to one hundred myself. Many years, I must use some of Madam MaRooska's staff to assist us, but hopefully I have equipped myself with enough extra help that I will not have to use her staff members. But to answer your initial question, there are a lot of local hotels in Northern Ireland. The participants will be staying in surrounding hotels, and they will drive in for the festivities and events. There are twenty-four-hour security and taxi services provided. There will also be shuttle buses provided by each hotel."

"I was reading over the Irish Times Newspaper this morning and found it very interesting that horse racing is intricately linked to Irish culture and has a long history on this Island," Lady Lindsey remarked.

"Yes," Lord Tutwiller agreed. "Horse racing is the most well-known spectator sport here in Ireland. We are strong in producing and training thoroughbred horses. We are very much like Great Britain. Our horses regularly compete and win in the British racing events."

"I also read..." Lady Lindsey interrupted. "...that the money was used to assist the rural economy of the country."

"Yes," Lord Tutwiller said. "Horse racing promotes business. Our Irish-bred horses dominate the highest levels internationally. Irish foals are exported to thirty different countries. We bring in millions of pounds annually from our sale of horses. The horse racing season kicks off during the Easter break with the Irvin Grand National Festival. There are festivals all over Ireland in which horses compete for the prize money. The horses who win become finalists for the Grand National Horse Race. This is the race that is held at our own Londonberry Estates in northern Ireland. This is the oldest race, and it is held at the end of the season."

"So, to even be eligible in this race, your horses and trainers must be spectacular?" Lady Lindsey observed.

"Precisely," Lord Tutwiller boasted. "And we have been hosting the National for the last ten years."

As they drove through the rolling hills of Londonberry Estates, the stadium and the white grandstands were very impressive. There was an oval racetrack in front of spectator stands. You could see the impressive racing stadium from miles away. You could see where the horses practiced before the grand race. The starting gate was set up and ready for the fifteen horses competing in the next race.

They arrived at Londonberry Estates, and Lord Tutwiller's limousine parked out front. The doorman came out to meet them. He escorted Lady Lindsey inside, and Lord Tutwiller followed. His estate was larger than Madam MaRooska's estate. He had two other buildings, which housed guests during horse races.

"We will have lunch," Lord Tutwiller said. "Lady Lindsey is not staying the night. I'm going to be showing her around the stables this afternoon."

"Yes, sir," the doorman replied. "I believe you all are expected in the grand dining hall."

Lady Lindsey and Lord Tutwiller made their way toward the grand dining hall. The room was elegant. The dining table was set. The linen tablecloths were woven with beading and embroidery from Paris. The chairs were covered in cut velvet upholstery, and the meals were served on gold-trimmed porcelain dinnerware. The drinks were served in crystal glasses with Lord Tutwillers's monogram on them. As Lady Lindsey and Lord Tutwiller sat down, the dinner was being served.

Lady Lindsey was impressed as she glanced around the dining hall. "And who are the people in these portraits?" she asked.

"I'm very proud to tell you that the collection of portraits is of the Lords of Ireland," Lord Tutwiller answered. "The title, 'The Lords of Ireland', was revised by Henry VIII. He changed the title of this collection to 'The Kings of Ireland.'"

When they were finished with the meal, Lord Tutwiller and Lady Lindsey walked around the room, viewing each portrait. Lord Tutwiller was immensely proud to give her the history of each portrait.

Then the doorman came to the room. "Your driver is here."

Lady Lindsey and Lord Tutwiller were driven out to the sporting arena. As they toured the facility, there was a lot of activity.

Lord Tutwiller was explaining procedures to Lady Lindsey as they walked. "Before the race, jockeys weigh out and report to the paddock for instructions by the trainers. By this time, the horses and riders proceed to the track in a parade for a brief warm-up gallop. The starting gates are electrically operated. The horses are walked to the starting gates." Lord Tutwiller was walking with Lady Lindsey. He was showing her what was going to happen when the race would begin. "The finish of the race is photographed by a special camera. The result of the race is not official until the jockeys are weighed in and post-race urine tests are made of the winning horses. If the results show the presence of forbidden substances, the results may be changed on the payments of horses, but not on bets."

After touring the rest of the facility, Lord Tutwiller suggested, "We'd best be going."

Lady Lindsey agreed, the limo driver was called, and they headed back toward Bellingfast Estates.

Lady Lindsey and Elizabeth Anne were in the library playing bridge. Reuben decided to call Charles Wolf to find out more details about the stolen currency. It took three tries before Reuben finally made the connection.

"Charles, Charles!" Reuben exclaimed. "I had to call you again to see if any more details about the stolen currency had come into your office."

"Yes," he responded. "The financial report for the last six months has finally come in. Six months ago, we were fine. Then, as the months passed, large amounts of money were drawn out each month. The financial statements had been falsely documented. So, I did not know until three months ago that the money had been withdrawn but not documented."

"Have you closed the account?" Reuben asked.

"Yes," Charles replied. "But, to my dismay, in studying the financial statement, I discovered your mother has only three million dollars left in the Caribbean stocks."

Reuben was very distressed, and he asked, "What can we do, Charles? What can we do?"

"I'm going to get my own private detective on this matter," Charles assured him. "I'm sure the money has not been spent and instead has been transferred to another account, but it'll take some offshore research to determine exactly which account it was designated into."

"I feel we still should not mention anything to Mama until we have more information," Reuben suggested.

"I wholeheartedly agree with you. We will just wait until we have more information."

At that, Reuben hung up the phone. He was neither relieved nor satisfied with the conversation, but at this time, there was nothing he could do.

Gina Dixon, a carefree college student from Paris, was walking with Sir Reggie Adams through the main hall. Virginia Camille was seated at a small table in the garden hall. She pretended to be enjoying the exotic plants and the marble and bronze sculptures in the room. Suddenly, she saw Gina and Sir Reggie as they walked across the polished marble floor.

Virginia Camille immediately approached Gina and Sir Reggie. "And where are you all going on this perky afternoon?"

Sir Reggie was pleased. He had already become interested in Virginia Camille at the masquerade ball. When she approached them, he was very intrigued. "We're going out for a game of golf. Virginia Camille, would you like to join us?"

Virginia looked at Gina, hoping for approval, "Why, yes, I would enjoy a game of golf. That is, if it is all right with you, Gina?" Gina looked at Sir Ralph and then replied, "Why, that would be fine."

At that, the three of them left the main hall and went out the front door. From there, a golf cart picked them up, and they were heading for the golf course, which was to the left of Bellingfast Estates.

By the time they arrived at the golf course, ten or so other persons were already on the course. The three went inside the clubhouse to get their golf clubs.

As they walked through the door, the man at the desk said, "Miss Dixon, you have a phone call. You can pick it up in the lobby."

"Please excuse me," Gina said. "I'll only be a minute. I'm sure it's my stage manager."

As she left for the lobby, Virginia Camille began to put on her southern charm. "Why, Sir Reggie...I was so hoping you and I would be paired together. When I saw you at the masquerade ball, I knew that out of all the men at the event, you had already tickled my fancy."

Sir Reggie looked around the room, grabbed Virginia Camille by the elbow, and kissed her on the lips. "I felt the same way when I saw you in the beautiful Marilyn Monroe white gown at the party. Why don't we get together later tonight after the golf game?" He winked.

Virginia Camille winked back and said, "I'll be counting the minutes."

As Gina walked back in from the lobby, she addressed both of them. "The phone call was my press agent. He has good news. He is lining me up for an interview for a new movie. We will be starting production at the first of the year. I am so excited. I've auditioned for the part of Cleopatra."

Later that afternoon, Lady Lindsey, Constance, and Virginia Camille were talking in the girl's room. Lady Lindsey had told them all about the visit to Londonberry Estates. Everybody was all excited about being involved with and attending the horse races, which would be held the next week at Londonberry Estates.

"Constance," Lady Lindsey said. "When are you to see Sir Hightower again?"

"Tonight, Lady Lindsey. Madam MaRooska has set us up to meet in the study. Madam MaRooska has planned for Sir Hightower, Edward Harper, Doctor Harriet Asbury, and myself to hold a seminar regarding the conclusion of my book. All these people are well-known in the literary world, and Madam MaRooska feels they could be of great help. So, that's what I have planned for tonight."

When Constance looked around, she noticed Virginia Camille, and she said, "Virginia Camille, would you like to come and observe while we discuss the conclusion of the book?"

"No, thank you," Virginia Camille answered. "I have plans."

"I hope you are planning on seeing that nice Doctor Wellington," Lady Lindsey remarked.

Virginia Camille smiled and walked into the salon area to fix her hair. Several hours passed, and Virginia Camille got her welcomed phone call from Sir Reggie Renaldo Adams.

"Yes, sounds great," she said into the phone. "I'll meet you in the lounge at 6:30. Thank you. I feel the same way about you."

Virginia Camille stretched out on the bed and began to dream about Sir Reggie Renaldo. There was just something intriguing and fascinating about those corrupt twins from Barbados. Virginia Camille also had a sneaky suspicion that these twins knew something about the mysterious appearance of the angel doll in her room. But how and why the doll fit into the puzzle of events were beyond her comprehension.

Meanwhile, Constance was quite excited about this first seminar with Edward Harper and Doctor Harriet Ashbury accompanied by Sir Hightower. Hopefully, she could get a clear and better insight on what would be a good ending for her book.

That night in the study, the four members of the seminar met in a room on the top floor. Madam MaRooska had chosen this room because it was a quiet and secluded. There would be no disturbances on this floor. The study was located on the east wing staircase. You had to climb a flight of winding stairs to get to this room.

As Constance entered the room, she commented, "That was an exhausting walk."

Sir Hightower got up and walked toward her to assist her. He gently led her to the long table to where the rest of the committee were seated. As she began to sit down, out of respect, Edward Levine Harper stood up until she was seated.

Doctor Ashbury remarked, “We were incredibly happy that Madam MaRooska set up this meeting for us.”

“She had given us specific details of your last visit, and she wanted us to share our best suggestions and possible conclusions on how to end your novel,” Edward Levine explained.

“I feel I need all the help I can get,” Constance said apologetically. “I was so upset about the situation from my last visit that I had a complete nervous breakdown. I haven’t been able to bring myself to even think about how to conclude this novel.”

Sir Hightower put his arm around Constance. “When we were on the trails together, I had no idea what all you had been through, but I know we can help you make the adjustment on a positive note. Our hope is that the conclusion will be just as meaningful and complete as the rest of your novel has been.”

“Madam MaRooska sent up tea and pastries,” said Doctor Ashbury. “Why don’t we enjoy the sweets together before we get started?”

Constance was beginning to feel more relaxed. She felt amazingly comfortable with this group of people who were going to make the transition for finishing her novel an easier project. Each one of the participants read over the content of the novel. Over the next hour, Doctor Ashbury and Edward Harper worked actively to try to connect the dots in order to make the conclusion more plausible. Sir Hightower worked with Constance, assisting her with her play-on words. He was trying to determine if something was a pun or simply a predestined prophecy. However, she wanted the reader to interpret as they wished. Constance asked many questions concerning the counterpart effectiveness of the main character. Edward and Doctor Ashbury made it clear that the cohesion of all the elements would come from Constance's development of the plot and how it related to the abstract theme of the story. After another hour or so, the group decided to break up. Constance thanked them graciously for their assistance.

As she and Sir Hightower walked down the winding stairway, Sir Hightower embraced Constance and kissed her with admiration.

He then looked in her eyes and said, "I think...I am falling in love."

They kissed again, and Constance went on her way downstairs. Sir Hightower went to his room, and Constance went to hers. Constance was incredibly happy. The night did seem to be very productive, and she now had enough courage to finish her novel.

Chapter 8

Romantic Rendezvous with Sir Reggie

Meanwhile, after primping in order to look her absolute best, Virginia Camille headed for the lounge to meet Sir Reggie Adams. When she walked into the lounge, Reggie was seated at the lounge bar with a cocktail in his hand. When he saw her coming in, he motioned for her to join him. She slowly strolled toward him, strutting leisurely with each step. When she got in front of his stool, she pretended to fix her shoelace, exposing her seductive breasts in her wide-open dress. He smiled. Sir Reggie pulled up a stool for her beside his, and he offered her a cocktail like the one he had ordered for himself. Being a Barbados playboy, Reggie was quite pleased with his conquest. After several more drinks and light conversation, he suggested they use a back staircase and enjoy the rest of the evening in his room. His brother was at Bellingfast Estates this evening, so they could be completely alone in his suite.

He and his brother had adjoining suites, numbers 216 and 217. These rooms were on the east wing of the building, so there would be no chance of running into Lady Lindsey or Constance. As they stepped into the room, Sir Reggie dimmed the lights and put on some romantic music. There was a bar in the room, and Sir Reggie delighted in mixing up more drinks as they began to leisurely stretch out on the reclining sofa. It circled around in a sitting room.

"Nice room, Sir Reggie," Virginia Camille noticed.

"It's nothing like the decor in room A," Sir Reggie responded. "I requested this room when I made my reservations. I had the concierge's office send me pictures. I knew I would probably be doing a lot of private negotiations while I was enjoying my stay at Bellingfast. Yes, I am quite pleased with this arrangement. I had Madam MaRooska send up several robes to be placed into the Boudoir chest. Check them out, so you will be comfortable."

While Virginia Camille was changing, Sir Reggie changed into a velvet brown robe with leather trim. Sir Reggie returned first to the reclining sofa. He had already made two more drinks. When Virginia Camille returned, she was taken aback by how very sophisticated and suave Sir Reggie appeared. He and his brother were both strikingly handsome men in their late forties or their early fifties. It was obvious that he knew how to entice the ladies. Virginia Camille was spellbound when she saw them at the masquerade ball. But she had learned that they could be corrupt and dangerous. That made her more eager to get to know them. Virginia Camille had been exposed to a lot of rich men, but only the adventuresome type could intrigue her enough to play the game of wits with them. Virginia Camille still believed that these men had something to do with the angel doll mystery. She did not yet understand how he was involved, but she had every intention of finding out.

"So, where is your brother tonight?" Virginia Camille asked.

"When I told him you were spending the evening with me, he suggested taking a room at Londonberry Estates."

"How convenient," Virginia Camille acknowledged.

"Yes, how convenient."

Then he pulled Virginia Camille over, and they made passionate love on the reclining sofa. They eventually wound up in the large bedroom and spent the rest of the night making love. The next morning, Virginia Camille had made her plans. As she got up, she cozied up to Sir Reggie and suggested that he go down to the dining hall and bring back breakfast for them to enjoy in the room together.

"I'll just call room service and have it sent up," he responded.

"Oh, no, Sir Reggie. I want you to specifically pick out my breakfast. I'm going to shower, and I'll be fresh when you return."

She bent over and kissed him passionately. He could not resist. He was very dominated by her sexuality and would do anything she desired.

Reggie got dressed and headed down to the dining hall. When he left the room, Virginia Camille watched him leave the room. Then she began to search. She knew there had to be some important documents in the room. She began to look through his wallet. Then she began to mess about with his computer. After ten minutes, Virginia Camille had unlocked some secret documents in a folder labeled "Angel Doll". Yes, she knew it was very mysterious, but at this time, she did not understand how this was to affect the family back in the United States. When she heard him coming, she quickly closed the computer, jumped into the bath, and asked Reggie to join her in the jacuzzi tub. Reggie felt he had made his conquest and was quite pleased with himself. He joined her in the tub.

As he was so infatuated with her sex appeal, it never occurred to him that she had ulterior motives for seducing him. He was enjoying it so much that he was caught offguard and played right into her hands. After enjoying the delicious breakfast, Virginia Camille dressed herself and promised that she would be back. Leaving his room, she knew she was on the right track and those dangerously corrupt Barbados men were playing with danger when Virginia Camille became involved in their schemes.

As Virginia Camille was going to her room, she passed by the breakfast room and saw Lady Lindsey and

Constance waiting to be served breakfast. She went directly to their table.

Constance was shocked to see her and said, "I got your text last night. I knew you were safe but had no idea who you were with."

Then Lady Lindsey chimed in. "I assumed you were with that nice Doctor Wellington. Were you with him?"

"Well, not exactly," Virginia Camille responded. "I'll tell you all about it when you two come upstairs."

Then Virginia Camille quickly ran upstairs. She did not want to be questioned anymore about her whereabouts or the information that she had acquired in Sir Reggie's room.

Thirty minutes passed. Lady Lindsey and Constance were quite interested in what Virginia Camille was going to share with them. As they entered the room, they saw that Virginia Camille had several documents to show them. Using her phone, she had taken pictures of about twelve documents full of data that were taken while Sir Reggie was gone to get her breakfast.

"So, who actually spent the night with you?" Lady Lindsey asked.

"Sir Reggie Renaldo Adams" was her answer.

"Oh, no!" Lady Lindsey and Constance shrieked at the same time.

"You could have been murdered!" Constance screamed. "I told you those men are corrupt and dangerous."

"Lord Tutwiller has been suspicious of them from the time they sent their confirmation of attendance to Madam MaRooska," Lady Lindsey explained. "We told you not to have anything to do with them."

"Never you mind!" Virginia Camille exclaimed. "Just look at the documents I copied while I was in his room."

As Constance and Lady Lindsey viewed the documents, they grew astonished.

"Why in the world would he have an 'Angel Doll' account in his name?" Lady Lindsey stammered. "And look. You'll notice there was another open account in Zurich, Switzerland. They added over twenty million dollars about two months ago. These men had transactions and accounts in Singapore and the Cayman Islands, all of which are labeled 'Angel Doll' accounts. They did not label where the twenty million came from."

Constance began to look closer at the documents. At the bottom of the transactions, there was some small fine print saying they were being backed by a large film corporation in Hollywood, California.

Constance came to a conclusion. "Somebody has stolen the rights to my book without me even knowing about it."

"That's what it looks like, my dear," Lady Lindsey sighed.

"So, what do we now?"

Chapter 9

Investigation of the Murder at Bellingfast

Later that afternoon, Bellingfast Estates were booming with activities. Metropolitan police from Scotland Yard were swarming all over the premises. A murder had been detected, and a female body had been found in the woods outside the riding trails that headed to the mountain view near the cliffs of Moher. The police officers were questioning everyone at Bellingfast.

Madam MaRooska assured the guests that the killer would be apprehended and that none of her guests were involved. Everybody was uneasy, but rumors about the strange occurrences at these events were quite publicized. All guests knew that when you came to Bellingfast, the character you chose could be very detrimental. You could encounter some of the same obstacles that the actual historical figure faced when he or she was alive.

That is why Madam MaRooska emphasized the importance of choosing one's character wisely because he or she could face dangerous obstacles while at the event. That was also why Madam MaRooska wanted each guest to be paired with a partner. This would always ensure a person's safety. Most of the guests were frightened. However, many guests enjoyed dabbling with danger. It was very adventurous and somewhat thrilling, and the guests wondered what would happen next.

Upon hearing about the murder, Madam MaRooska immediately planned a meeting with all the staff members at Bellingfast Estates in the kitchen. All the staff members were present.

"I regret to inform you all that another tragic incident has taken place. Scotland Yard police will be on the premises for several days. They will be asking questions to solve the mystery. Please inform all the other guests that this is just a routine investigation. Do not be alarmed, but do try to be cooperative with the police. If any of the guests are overly concerned, have them come talk with me. Any questions? If not, you are dismissed."

Gladys Hartfield had only been with Madam MaRooska for a few months. Prior to her employment, she had been with Lord Tutwiller, who owned Londonberry Estates. Londonberry Estates were home to a neighboring castle. Gladys grew up at Londonberry Estates, as Gladys' mother had worked with Lord Tutwiller as the head housekeeper. When her mother died, there was no question as to who would inherit the head housekeeper's position. There was no animosity, but when Madam

MaRooska began to have extremely wealthy and distinguished guests from around the world attend, Gladys began to look to Bellingfast Estates for employment. She wanted to be a part of all the fun, excitement, and adventure of working there. Gladys was a little envious and jealous of all the exciting things that went on there, so when the position became available, Gladys quickly applied and automatically got the job. She became the head housekeeper at Madam MaRooska's famous estate in Belfast, Ireland.

Lord Tutwiller did not object. He wanted a much younger woman to run his household estate, so when Gladys Hartfield asked about her resignation, he excitedly agreed to let her leave. Sissily and Gladys were very much accustomed to the strange events that went on at Bellingfast Estates. Strange disappearances and unexplainable deaths were quite common. However, no one had ever been arrested or convicted. The rumors were very much publicized. So, when an individual made a reservation at Madam MaRooska's famous resort, they were aware of the possible dangers that they may encounter. Most guests were more intrigued with the adventure and excitement of the two-week encounter at the famous resort than they were afraid. Her guests were some of the richest and most stimulating persons from around the globe. It was just the opportunity to be in the presence of these kinds of people that made the two to three year waits much more plausible.

Inspector Barnes and Inspector Gibbs were assigned to the case. Inspector Barnes was aware of what was going on. He had been sent to Belfast on several occasions regarding unexplainable mysteries.

"Is this your first time at Bellingfast Estates?" Inspector Barnes asked.

"Yes, I've always wanted to be assigned, but I've never been asked." Inspector Gibbs replied.

"Well, it is exceedingly difficult to solve these mysteries. I've been on three cases, and no conclusions were ever disclosed."

"What is so hard?" Inspector Gibbs asked.

"These cases always lead to dead ends," said Inspector Barnes. "And Scotland Yard just simply drops the cases."

"Do you think they are inside jobs?"

"They could be, but nobody can ever prove a thing," Inspector Barnes said. "Well, we had better get started."

"We do have a lot of work to do for the next couple of days. I have a list of guests here at Bellingfast. Why don't we divide the list up? You take half and I will take the other half."

"Sounds good to me, but we need a full account of what each person has been doing for the last couple of days. We will need to follow up on any suspicious activity."

Inspector Barnes divided the list, and they started right away. When he entered the garden room, Lady Lindsey, Virginia Camille, and Constance were chatting at a small table. Approaching the ladies, he discovered that they were on his list. All three ladies had explicit details on where they had been for the past two days. Lady Lindsey had left the estate to be with Lord Tutwiller. Of course, Constance spent the night in a cave overnight near the cliffs of Moher. Virginia Camille had not left the estate. The three ladies were in the clear.

Inspector Barnes was extremely interested in the Barbados twins. These men just appeared suspicious to the inspector. He figured the twins were in the building. Asking around, he found out that they were in the library. When he approached them in the library, they were very calm and relaxed. Each man began to explain his whereabouts for the past two days.

Then Inspector Barnes asked about the nights. "Have you all got alibis for the night hours?"

"Why, yes, we were in our room all night long, both nights. We were reading. We enjoy checking out the novels from the library and comparing notes on specific authors."

How interesting, Inspector Barnes thought to himself. How interesting and a nice alibi.

After checking with several more guests and staff members, the police officers left Bellingfast and went to the police station. By this point, a full report had come in about the corpse. The body was that of a woman. It looked like she had been strangled. It could have even been a suicide because of the bruising around the neck. This information would aid the inspectors. It was determined that the woman had died at night in the early hours right before dawn.

Sir Callahan and Sir Richardson had talked to most of the guests, sharing the information that Madam Ma-Rooska had given to them. Sissily walked into the main hall and approached the front desk. Sir Callahan and Sir Richardson were talking.

As she stood in front of the desk, she couldn't help being very inquisitive. "Have either of you men seen the countess?"

"Do you mean Countess Christina Anderson from Scotland?" Sir Callahan inquired.

"Yes, that's precisely who I'm talking about. Mrs. Hatfield and I have observed that she has not slept in her room for the last two nights."

"Hmm, I will ask around," Sir Richardson remarked. "Maybe she had business in town."

Sissily looked puzzled. "You don't think she was the person who was murdered?"

"Of course not, who would want to murder the countess?"

I do not know, but it is strange to me, Sir Callahan then thought to himself. It is strange, because the countess, Constance, Sir Hightower, and Sir Ralph Grantly Adams were the guests who spent the night in the cave near the cliffs of Moher. Then the terrible storm blew through. I do wonder if there could be a connection.

The next day, two inspectors and a deputy commissioner returned to Bellingfast Estates to continue the questioning of the guests. However, this time, they knew the woman had been murdered at night. They were able to pinpoint the relative time of the death. It had happened at approximately 4:00 AM. As they walked through the front entrance, Madam MaRooska met them at the door. Deputy Commissioner Stewart Menzies was pleased that the coroner's report had come in. This added information that would help solve the case.

Madam MaRooska and the three men went right to the study. The study was perhaps one of the most interesting rooms in the castle. It was on the top floor on the last wing of the castle. The paneling was made from teakwood and cherry. It was an awfully expensive wood that had been salvaged from the Orient. The wood had a brass glaze applied to it to give it a highlighted appearance. Brass shelves ran parallel on the two-shelved walls of the study. Volumes and volumes of analytical critiques were displayed on the shelves. Every author who had made a notable contribution was recognized for his research and talent.

As they entered the room, the police officers and Madam MaRooska sat down around the big desk.

"We found information concerning the death," Deputy Commissioner Stewart Menzies explained. "Either the woman was strangled or it was a knife stabbing because of the bruising on the neck. The time of death has been determined to be around 4:00 AM. So, the suspect had to have left the building early in the morning. Her body had been on the grounds for over twenty-four hours. We do not know where she was strangled or stabbed. Have all your guests been accounted for?"

"I think so," Madam MaRooska answered. "But I can't be one hundred percent sure."

"Well, you will need to come to the coroner's office to identify the corpse," Inspector Gibbs responded. "If she is a guest here at Bellingfast Estates, we will need to notify her family."

Then Madam MaRooska said, "I'll go with you gentlemen to the coroner's office."

At this, the four of them left Bellingfast Estates.

When they arrived at the coroner's office, they were led directly to the body. The room was very large and cold. In the middle of the room was a table with the body under a sheet. As they walked toward it, Madam MaRooska was very apprehensive about looking at the body. Her staff had verified to her that they thought all guests had been accounted for, but they were not one hundred percent sure. The man in the long white cotton jacket pulled back the sheet, and Madam MaRooska gazed at the corpse. She immediately recognized Countess Christina from Scotland.

"Yes, I do recognize her," Madam MaRooska acknowledged. "She is a guest at the resort. Countess Christina Anderson. My staff thought all the guests had been accounted for, but they were clearly mistaken. When I return to Bellingfast, I will call you and give you the details on how to reach her family."

The officers were incredibly pleased that the body had been identified. The deputy commissioner and the two detectives, along with Madam MaRooska, left the office and returned to Bellingfast Estates. The ride back to the estates was noticeably quiet. Another tragic event had happened at Madam MaRooska's Specialty Resort, and she was reeling.

By the time the car arrived at Bellingfast, the word was out. Yes, the murdered body had been a guest at

Bellingfast. It was obvious upon arrival that all the guests had been notified of the tragic incident. The two detectives told Madam MaRooska that they would be back the next day and that they needed to start a full investigation. As Madam MaRooska walked through the front door, she had to work hard to maintain her composure. Strange events did occur, and most were never solved or explained.

Putting a smile on her face, she resumed her duties of being the ideal hostess at her world-renowned resort for the rich and famous. It was hard to understand, but the strange events that happened made a stay at Bellingfast much more intriguing for the guests. That is why so many people wanted to go to her parties. Regardless of the danger, the whole resort was talking about the mysterious murder of the countess.

Who would want to kill her? What would be the purpose of the death?

Back in the kitchen, the staff was trying to explore all possibilities for the tragic occurrence. Gertrude was very much engaged in conversation with Sir Callahan and Sir Richardson.

"We do not know who did this treacherous act, but I agree with Madam MaRooska. I have been suspicious of those Barbados twins from the time they sent in their confirmation papers."

"I agree," Sir Callahan stated.

"I recollect everything," Gertrude acknowledged that fact. "When I received her call, I tried to acquire personal information on the men. Sissily reprimanded me because the Madam had emphatically instructed us not to inquire into personal files. However, I see now that was a mistake. We needed to disclose any negative information about those men, because, as we thought, they are dangerous."

"I agree, Gertrude," Sir Richardson stated. "But what can we do now? It's too late. I just hope that the investigation goes quickly, and the murder is solved."

"Indeed," Sir Callahan remarked. "What could be worse than an unsolved murder?"

"Two unsolved murders," Gertrude answered vehemently. "I must get on back to work. This situation has affected us all, but I must contain myself and get on with my obligations."

Early the next morning, the Scotland Yard detectives were ready to start a full investigation concerning the murder of Countess Christina Langley Stewart.

Inspector Barnes instructed Inspector Gibbs, "Today we will conduct a complete investigation of Bellingfast Estates. This includes the total building."

"Yes," Inspector Gibbs replied. "We have talked to most of the guests here at the resort. You are correct. We have not searched the building itself yet."

"Let's go together," Inspector Barnes suggested. "You take notes, and we will search for any signs or observations."

"Good idea," Inspector Gibbs answered. "Good idea."

"Let us take the elevator down to the basement. We need to be looking in inconspicuous places," Inspector Barnes suggested.

"Yes," Inspector Gibbs added. "We should be looking for a very private and secretive area, which would probably go unnoticed in a routine check."

"What kind of details are you looking for?" asked Inspector Barnes.

"Anything that looks out of the ordinary, you know," stated Inspector Gibbs. "Anything that looks out of place."

Once they got to the basement, they wandered into the cellar. There were rows and rows of boxes. Inspector Gibbs opened several of the boxes. Most of the boxes contained the same things: linens, towels, sheets, and pillowcases. The linens did not look like they had been used. However, Inspector Gibbs was quite shocked when he opened the smallest box. He saw dolls, dolls, and more dolls. Inspector Gibbs called for Inspector Barnes to come see what he had found.

"Do you recognize this doll?" Inspector Gibbs asked.

Inspector Barnes gasped. Both men nearly fell to the floor with shock.

Everyone that worked at Scotland Yard knew about the murder that had taken place three years before at Londonberry Estates. A woman had been severely mutilated. Hearsay was that she had stolen the doll from Constance Stallings, and the doll possessed magnificent powers.

"We have a lot to talk about back at headquarters," Inspector Barnes said. "Something fishy is going on. I do not know heads or tails about what it means, but I do know it must be in connection with the murder from

Londonberry Estates three years ago."

As Inspector Gibbs was picking up the box, he noticed a bloody rag inside. He found another doll. This one was coated with blood.

"Good grief." Inspector Barnes grabbed the box and found a knife, bloody cloth, and the dolls. He then crammed the knife and bloody doll back into the box with the others. "We must get to headquarters before somebody sees us."

The men hastened outside the building. They entered their police car and sped to Scotland Yard headquarters.

Inside Scotland Yard, the commissioner and the deputy commissioner were remarkably busy. The headquarters had been buzzing with activity. With the Grand National festivals going on in Dublin and the final Grand National Horse Race going on at Londonberry, the city was booming with activity. People were flying in from all over the globe to attend the horse races. Corruption and crime were rampant. Scotland Yard policemen had been running all over Ireland, trying to solve the crime and corruption as they occurred.

Inspector Barnes stepped into the front office. "Excuse me, excuse me," he said.

"Yes?" the commissioner responded.

"We need to talk to you about an urgent matter," Inspector Barnes explained.

"Yes, do come in and tell us about it," the commissioner instructed.

Inspector Barnes explained his reluctance to talk before the whole group.

"Don't worry," the commissioner reassured him. "These men are all trustworthy."

"Well, okay, let me call Inspector Gibbs to bring the box to the front office," explained Inspector Barnes.

All the police officers greeted Inspector Gibbs when he came in with the box.

"What have you got here?" another deputy commissioner inquired.

"Well..." Inspector Barnes answered. "See for yourself."

Inspector Gibbs put the box on the table. The deputy assistant commissioner slowly opened the box. He removed the cloth and revealed the contents of the box. As the men peered into the box, they became horrified. All the officers distinctly remembered the murder at Londonberry Estates three years prior and remembered what the doll looked like.

Then the commissioner, who was head of Scotland Yard, asked Inspector Gibbs, "Do you think there is any connection between the dolls and the murder of the countess from Scotland?"

"I really cannot see any connection at this time," Gibbs replied.

"However," Inspector Barnes added. "We just found the dolls today. So, currently, we have no conclusive evidence to connect the two murders."

The commissioner then replied, "Let us keep the box of dolls here on file. We can get blood samples from the bloody cloth that is wrapped around the dolls and from the knife."

“Come on, Inspector Gibbs,” Inspector Barnes suggested. “Let us get back to Bellingfast. This finding has provided us with new facts concerning the murder.”

The two men left the headquarters and rode back to Bellingfast to continue the investigation. Meanwhile, the police officers at Scotland Yard talked among themselves.

“This is one of the strangest cases I’ve ever heard of in all of my thirty years here at Scotland Yards,” the commissioner said.

When the men opened the box to examine the contents, they found five little dolls, one of which was bloody, and a knife inside a bloody cloth. The deputy commissioner recollected the dolls immediately. He went to his files and pulled out a picture with a description below it. He then compared the dolls in the box with the snapshot of the doll from three years before.

Yes, the dolls looked identical.

The doll was hand-carved from cypress wood. Cypress trees were prominent in the Louisiana Bayou. There were little legs and arms, which extended from the body. Tiny hooks and screws attached the limbs to the body frame. The wood was painted with dye made from wild berries. The clothing was made from old scraps of material.

After looking in the box, the commissioner realized that the five unbloodied dolls were made from birch wood, which was from a softwood tree found in Ireland, so the bodies of the five dolls were different from the original angel doll from Louisiana. The bodies were made from different woods.

The commissioner was troubled over this finding. He was aware of the legend about the angel doll. However, three years before, the housekeeper at Londonberry Estates had stolen the angel doll from Constance. Constance was trying to finish the last three chapters of her novel when it was stolen. There was an ancient legend of the slaves in Southern Louisiana. They believed that possession of an angel doll at one's death would cause them to reappear in the next life as a person of a different race. Death would cause a Negro to return as a Caucasian. No one in south Louisiana believed the old Negro legend. When the housekeeper was found mutilated in the basement at Londonberry Estates, she was holding an angel doll in her hand. Her body was unrecognizable, but dental records confirmed that she was the victim. Everyone knew that the housekeeper was a Negro. When the pathologist report came back, all DNA testing showed that the body was that of a Caucasian woman in her late fifties, the same age as the housekeeper.

When Constance was in Bellingfast the first time, one of the guests in attendance was a screenwriter and movie producer. He kept an exceptionally low profile. When the murder at Londonberry took place, he knew that a perfect movie could be in the making. Shortly after the murder occurred, the information spread like wildfire, and all of Northern Ireland was interested in the angel doll legend. The screenwriter used his prominence and connections in the film world to steal a copy of the novel. However, the last three chapters were incomplete.

Upon finding this intriguing script, the movie producer quickly notified the most established film production company in Hollywood, and the movie was underway. It was an unofficial stolen copyright, even though the book was not published. The film director had been hired, and actors and actresses were auditioning for parts.

What complicated matters was that now, three years later, the author of The Angel Doll was making her final visit to Bellingfast to finish her last three chapters. The filming company had changed the name of the film, but the storyline was identical. They knew that the public finding out about them stealing someone else's narrative idea could put them in hot water, so they discreetly planned to have Constance murdered while she was finishing the last three chapters of the book. That would eliminate the potential for the real author to come forward, and the movie company could continue with their plan.

However, they had to find a way to be at Bellingfast while Constance was there. The biggest problem was finding the right person to carry out the murder. Secrecy was an absolute imperative. There could be no trace of this incident being blamed on the filming company.

Over the years, many unethical dealings had been spearheaded by major film companies in Hollywood. The ambassador of Barbados was deeply knowledgeable of the corrupt dealings that movie companies had been involved in. On several occasions, the ambassador of Barbados had rendered his services for a lofty amount of money. When the filming company made contact with the ambassador, the ambassador was pleased to offer his services. His two nephews were perfect candidates for this assignment. The two young men, Reggie Renaldo Adams and Ralph Grantly Adams, made their reservations at Madam MaRooska's famous resort. The ambassador knew that these men could complete the assignment very discreetly and unobtrusively.

The deputy commissioner asked, "What do we do now? It is strange that the previous murder happened at Londonberry Estates, but the dolls were found at Bellingfast."

"How can these two estates be connected?" another officer questioned.

The deputy commissioner addressed the situation. "There must have been somebody who had access to both estates."

"You are right," the officer responded. "Madam MaRooska and Lord Tutwiller have been close friends for many years. On many occasions, Madam MaRooska's staff would be used at Lord Tutwiller's estate when special events would be held. Therefore, most of the employees at Bellingfast were familiar with the employees at Londonberry Estates."

"But..." the deputy commissioner said, attempting to steer everyone back to the main question. "What about the recent murder at Bellingfast, the murder of Countess Christina from Scotland? How is her murder related to the murder of the housekeeper three years ago at Londonberry?"

Later that afternoon, Inspector Gibbs and Inspector Barnes were back at Bellingfast Estates. This new evidence, the box of angel dolls, had opened up a new line of questioning. Sir Callahan, Sir Richardson, Gertrude, Sissily, and Gladys Hatfield were in the maid's kitchen.

"What do you think he wants this time?" Gertrude asked, and then she gulped. "They have already questioned us for hours regarding this matter."

"Just routine," Sir Callahan responded. "They have to do their job. If it takes questions over and over, they will do it."

Gladys Hatfield looked at Scissily, "Well, I don't like it. I've got my own work to do."

Sir Richardson looked at his watch. "They said they would be here around 3 o'clock."

A phone call came into the maid's kitchen.

Sissily answered it. "Hello? Yes, fine, send them on down. We are all in the kitchen."

Sir Callahan and Sir Richardson were very well-accustomed to the investigation process of any criminal activity at Bellingfast Estates. They were not annoyed one bit. These men were always pleasant and cooperated with the Scotland Yard's police any time they were in the building. Their line of questioning was somewhat different from the first investigation earlier in the week.

When the police entered the room, all the employees were standing.

"Please be seated," Inspector Barnes directed.

All five staff members sat down at the table. Inspector Barnes was on one end of the table, and Inspector Gibbs was on the other end. All the staff at Bellingfast had enjoyed some of the work they had done at Londonberry. Madam MaRooska had always offered her custodial staff to assist Lord Tutwiller at the special events.

Inspector Barnes started the questioning by asking each employee how long he or she had worked at Bellingfast Estates.

"Well," Sir Callahan answered. "Madam MaRooska opened the inn. I had been employed at another hotel near Londonberry. Sir Richardson and I had been buddies since high school. When Sir Richardson was offered a job at Bishop's Gate, he talked with the manager, and I got on as a desk clerk. We both were employed at Bishop's Gate Hotel outside Londonberry. Then Madam MaRooska opened Bellingfast Estates. We both were highly recommended by the United Kingdom Hotel commissioner in Ireland. We both have been with Madam MaRooska since it was opened."

Gertrude spoke up next. "My family is from Dublin. My ancestors had worked at Kylemorre Abbey in Galway when she opened the resort. She specifically called Kylemorre Abbey and asked for an employee. I was highly recommended. My family was highly respected. We had worked for a great national leader, Lord Edward Fitzgerald."

"That's enough now for you two ladies. Tell me about your credentials and references."

Gladys Hatfield responded next. "Well, Inspector Barnes, my mum worked at Londonberry Estates her entire life. When my mum died, Lord Tutwiller hired me to take her place. I stayed with him up until two years ago when I was employed to work at Bellingfast."

The detective asked, "Why did you leave? Were you fired?"

"No, sir, Lord Tutwiller was pleased with my work. I was just ready for a change."

The men looked at each other. They knew that was a strange coincidence because now it was apparent that Gladys was at Londonberry Estates three years before when the murder took place. Gladys did not mention one word about the incident.

"Young lady, tell me about yourself," the deputy commissioner said to Sissily.

"I met Madam MaRooska a few years back. I was working in New York City at the Waldorf Astoria. My nephew was hired at Bellingfast Estates as a riding instructor."

"Where is your home?" Inspector Gibbs asked.

"New York," she answered.

"No, where was your residence before you worked at The Waldorf?" Inspector Gibbs interjected.

"Oh, my nephew and I are both from Lafayette, Louisiana, in the states," she replied.

Inspector Barnes looked immediately at Inspector Gibbs. There was the connection. Both people were from Lafayette, Louisiana. The angel doll had belonged to Constance Stallings, and she too had connections to Louisiana.

As the detectives were making their final report, they felt very suspicious of these people. Gladys Hatfield was working at Londonberry Estates when the murder occurred, and now two more suspects could be connected by their association.

Lord Tutwiller arrived at Scotland Yard's headquarters at the request of Sir Basil Thomson and Deputy Commissioner Stewart Menzies. They had called him in for questioning. Lord Tutwiller had been a longtime friend of Scotland Yard's police force.

"Lord Tutwiller," Sir Basil Thomson said. "You know we have the Barbados twins in custody. They have been in jail for two days."

"Yes, I am well aware of their reputations and their criminal offenses," Lord Tutwiller replied.

"We have confiscated their computer, and we have been able to surmise from the computer that their business dealings had been criminal and corrupt. However, just from the computer analysis, we cannot prove that these men are responsible for the murder of Countess Christina Langley Andrews from Scotland."

"What do you mean?" Lord Tutwiller asked.

Then the commissioner, Sir Basil Thomson, asked Stewart Menzies to bring in the box that Gibbs and Barnes had brought in two days ago. "Open the box, Lord Tutwiller, and we will explain," he requested.

As Lord Tutwiller opened the box, he was astonished. Seeing those angel dolls simply blew his mind.

As the story went, Constance Stallings grew up in a very wealthy family from Bastrop, Louisiana. Her family owned a plantation called Parkview Plantation with hundreds of acres of cotton, soybeans, and sugar cane fields. Constance was raised by her two aunts, Lady Lindsey and Glenora Stallings. Constance's mother was very much an aristocrat, and she spent most of her life traveling abroad, enjoying the extravagant sights. As children, Constance and her cousin Virginia Camille spent each summer in and around the plantation home. Many rich farmers lived in this part of Louisiana, from Baton Rouge and Lafayette.

"I do not know how she got the angel doll," the commissioner said. "However, Constance, Virginia Camille, and the Negro children on the plantation played together. They always played with the little doll. It was a simple little doll made from cypress wood from the cypress swamps in Southern Louisiana. It was about the size of a toothbrush. It had carved legs and arms. The doll was painted with dyes made from wild berries. The dress was made from leftover quilt material. When Constance was persuaded to go to Ireland to finish the last three chapters of her book, she enthusiastically agreed to go. Madam MaRooska had writers, scientists, theologians, politicians, and many other professions at her events, so Constance knew the people at this resort could inspire her to finish the last chapters of her book. So, she got her passport and made her first journey to Ireland."

"As you recall," Sir Basil Thomson reminded Lord Tutwiller. "One of your domestic staff, a Negro maid, was found mutilated in the basement at Londonberry Estates."

"Yes, I well recall the tragic event. It was a horrific death," Deputy Commissioner Stewart Menzies said, continuing the story. "Also, as you recall, when the body was examined at the coroner's office, the DNA results showed that the Negro maid was Caucasian. Legend had it that the one who possessed the angel doll at the time of their death would be transformed into another race."

"Of course, Lord Tutwiller," Sir Basil said. "None of us at Scotland Yard believed this mysterious tale."

Lord Tutwiller added, "I do not think any of my staff believed the story either."

"However," the commissioner continued. "The angel doll was found in your basement at Londonberry Estates with the corpse."

Lord Tutwiller agreed. "After the autopsy and crime report were completed, the angel doll was sent back to Bastrop, Louisiana, to Constance Stallings. There was no doubt about it, the Negro maid had all signs, blood work, and even hair follicles of a Caucasian woman in her fifties. The same age as the Negro woman, but a different race."

"Yes, that was very strange," Lord Tutwiller admitted. "It was very strange."

Then the deputy commissioner directed Lord Tutwiller to closely observe the angel dolls in the box.

As the three men investigated the box, they began to compare the pictures of the original angel doll to the copied dolls. The doll bodies from the box were made from the birch tree wood. The clothing was similarly made of scraps of cloth.

The commissioner said to Deputy Commissioner Menzies, "Go get the bloody cloth and knife."

Deputy Commissioner Menzies left the room and returned with two clear plastic bags. One contained the bloody knife. The other contained the bloody cloth that was found wrapped around one of the dolls. Lord Tutwiller was eager to hear the explanation of the contents of plastic bags.

"We took both of the plastic bags to the coroner's office when the body of Countess Christina came in," explained Commissioner Sir Basil Thomson. "After a thorough examination of the corpse of the countess, it was proved that the countess was stabbed in the heart with this knife. Now, how the bloody cloth fits into the picture could not be determined."

"That is very interesting," Lord Tutwiller admitted. "And how and what is the correlation between the countess's murder and the angel dolls found at Bellingfast Estates?"

"However," the deputy commissioner said. "We will have to let the Barbados twins out of jail pretty soon."

"What do you mean?" asked Lord Tutwiller.

"Well, we confiscated their computers, and we found a lot of criminal activities and associations, but the fingerprints on the knife did not match either of the twins."

"I am very surprised," Lord Tutwiller said. "I could have sworn they were involved in the mysterious murder of Countess Christina Andrews."

It was a fact that neither twin could be indicted on murder with this evidence alone.

"Now, let me address another matter," Sir Basil Thomson began. "Tell me about Gladys Hatfield."

"Do you think she has anything to do with the murder?" Lord Tutwiller questioned.

"Well, we do not know," the commissioner replied. "We must follow all leads on the matter."

Sir Basil continued talking. "Inspector Barnes has been involved with this case. He had questioned all of Madam MaRooska's domestic help, and he did find out that Gladys Hatfield was working for you three years ago. Gladys was a hard worker. Her mum had worked for thirty years, and Gladys grew up at Londonberry Estates. She was raised on the property. Everybody liked her."

"Why did she leave you?" asked the commissioner.

"Well, it was strange. About a year after the murder took place, she said she was ready for a change. So, she requested to be moved to Madam MaRooska's Specialty Resort. Her mum had died several years before, and I just think she wanted a change. What is your connection?"

"Well, somebody somewhere tried to duplicate Constance Stallings' The Angel Doll," the commissioner explained.

"For what purpose?" Lord Tutwiller asked.

"We do not know, but we are going to find out."

Then Lord Tutwiller reassured the commissioner, "I'm sure Gladys is not involved in any criminal activity. As for the Barbados twins, that is a different matter altogether." Then Lord Tutwiller stood up and said, "Gentlemen, have I answered your questions sufficiently?"

"Yes, thank you, Lord Tutwiller. We'll keep you informed."

The commissioner, deputy commissioner, and the detectives were going over the fine details in the printout that they got from the Barbados twins' computer. The computers had been returned to the men, but the composite transcript was printed for evidence. Each commissioner had been given their own copy to study carefully and precisely. They were looking for any information about illegal transactions or information concerning the murder of the countess. The transcript had no mention of the author. The first ten pages indicated that a specific amount of money had been deposited. Then they noticed that accounts had been moved from the Cayman Islands. Quite a lot of money had been transferred from one account, Singapore Trust, to another. The last observation was that on a specific date the previous year, there was money in The Bank of Zurich in Switzerland in the amount of ten million dollars.

The commissioners noticed a discrepancy about the author of the book. The Angel Doll's author had been identified as Constance Stallings. Now, when the account was changed to Switzerland, the name "Constance Stallings" was removed, and the name "Countess Christina Langley Anderson" was substituted. This was a strange entry because the actual murder plot was to kill Constance Stallings. The names had been swapped in the transcript. After the author's name was changed to "Countess Christina Langley Anderson", some suspicions arose. Several questions remained about the murder and mutilation at Londonberry Estates. The victim had the angel doll in her possession. Nobody was ever identified as the murderer in that case. The case was eventually listed as unsolved.

The prior murder left a great deal of questions unanswered, and now these angel dolls reappeared at Bellingfast Estates. This left the commissioners with questions to the motives of each murder.

"Something sounds very fishy to me," the commissioner said. "Movie studios have been known to steal movie rights by changing the copyright information before the book or proposed movie has been solicited."

"That would explain the money component of the whole situation," the deputy commissioner replied. "The book was to be released as nonfiction, and people from all over the world would be interested in its contents."

"Yes," the commissioner added. "The movie studio in Hollywood supplied the money."

Both men pondered this.

"So how does the death of the countess fit into this plot?" asked the deputy commissioner.

"It is obvious now," the commissioner answered. "Constance Stallings was the intended victim, but the killer or killers murdered the wrong person. Who would benefit from the Countess being eliminated?"

Suddenly, everybody in the room intuitively deduced that the earl of Scotland would be the benefactor of anything that belonged to his wife, Countess Christina. On the computer printout, Countess Christina Langley Andrews was the author of *The Angel Doll.* The earl had dealings with the twins in the past. He knew the twins were very competent. The earl knew that his wife was going to Madam MaRooska's Specialty Resort for two weeks. Information had been leaking all over London that the earl of Scotland had been stealing money from Countess Christina's trust account for well over two years. Countess Christina was now ready to confront her husband with the illegal confiscation of money from her trust fund. When the earl of Scotland found out what Christina was planning, he knew he had to make his own plans and have her murdered.

The earl was very much informed about the situation. He knew that Constance Stallings would be at Madam MaRooska's Specialty Resort at the same time his wife, the countess, would be there. The earl also knew that the Barbados twins had been sent to Bellingfast Estates to carry out Constance's murder. The movie studio had already stolen the copyright of the book, but the only way they could legally claim the royalties was for Constance to be eliminated completely, body and name. That was the purpose of the Barbados twins going to Bellingfast Estates.

"I figure we could use the Scotland Yard security system to aid in solving this murder," Sir Basil Thomson suggested.

"Yes," Commissioner Steward Menzies agreed. "I know we have those resources, but we hate to invade the privacy of her guests."

"When we installed the security system three years ago, we knew it would be beneficial in solving the numerous crimes and murders that had taken place over the years," Sir Basil explained.

"What do you think?" Commissioner Menzies asked.

"Why don't we open up the tapes and see if anything can be revealed?" Sir Thomson said.

"How many clocks have the security system installed?" Commissioner Stewart Menzies inquired.

"Seven or eight? I'm not sure," Sir Basil responded. "However, if we review the tapes, I'm sure we can find something that will help us."

Sir Basil Thomson and Stewart Menzies spent the remainder of the afternoon reviewing all recorded tapes from the last few days. The tapes were easy to understand. When there was no conversation, the tapes did not run. Only when conversation occurred would the tapes record any activity.

The tapes revealed that Gertrude and Gladys Hatfield had been running their own business right out the basement of Bellingfast Estates. They were involved in producing and selling angel dolls. These dolls were replicas of the doll found at Londonberry Estates three years prior. These two women had a very lucrative business. However, when the dolls were found in the wine cellar, the Scotland Yard's police made this connection. The bloody doll and knife must have been connected to the murder scheme.

•••

Reuben glanced at his phone and noticed that Charles Wolf had been trying for the past twenty-four hours to reach him.

It must be important, Reuben thought to himself.

Reuben knew that Lady Lindsey and Elizabeth Anne were dining together, so he felt very safe in returning Mr. Wolf's phone call.

"What have you found out, Charles? I just received your message. I knew it had to be especially important and urgent."

"Yes, Reuben. As you recall from our last conversation, I told you I was going to get my private investigators on the matter."

"Yes, I do remember," Reuben answered.

"Well, my men found out plenty of information! It all pertains to money that has been illegally transferred from your mother's account to offshore companies. These companies are using her money for illegal gambling and drugs."

"I can't believe this," Reuben was astonished. "How would this be going on and we didn't suspect a thing?"

Charles continued. "Now, listen to this. The Barbados twins are imposters. They are at Madam MaRooska's Specialty Resort right now. These two men are hired criminals. They have been working for an underground organization. They have confiscated large amounts of money. They have railroaded the money into gambling and mafia type activities."

"What do you mean?" Reuben asked.

"These men have contacts in the film and theatre industries from Los Angeles to New York. As a matter of fact, these men have already stolen the movie rights from the latest novel that Constance Stallings has not even finished yet."

"I must sit down," Reuben stammered. "I am devastated about this. Our family has never been involved with a situation like this."

"Well, Reuben," said Mr. Wolf. "I agree with the authorities from Scotland Yard. Mysterious occurrences happen at that resort. No one has ever been arrested, but numerous unexplained deaths seem to constantly occur, and huge amounts of money seem to disappear from many guests. Nobody has ever been arrested. The mysteries have not been solved. Take my word. Take my word, Reuben D'La Chaisson, that is a dangerous place to go."

"So, what can we do?" Reuben asked fretfully.

"Just be careful," Charles explained. "And take my word that those Barbados twins are criminals. Don't say anything to anyone. I will contact you later with our plan of action. Again, these men are criminals, and they will stop at nothing. And yes, Reuben, both men have been to the penitentiary. They have had plenty of contact with underground criminals. Just be careful, and I'll contact you soon."

About that time, Elizabeth Ann and Lady Lindsey entered the room.

"Hello, darling," Elizabeth Ann addressed Reuben. She put her arms around him and kissed him.

"Oh, hello, dear. Did you have a good lunch?" Reuben asked.

"Yes," Lady Lindsey responded. "It was very nice."

The two ladies sat down.

"Reuben," Lady Lindsey began. "I am really worried about this last occurrence."

"Do you mean the murder of the countess?"

"Yes, absolutely," Lady Lindsey acknowledged.

"I am worried about my own safety," Elizabeth Ann added.

"As a matter of fact," Lady Lindsey acknowledged. "I feel many guests at Madam MaRooska's Specialty Resort are somewhat frightened."

Reuben was still trying to grasp an understanding of the subject matter of his call to Charles Wolf. He had a very puzzled look on his face.

"Did you hear me, Reuben?!" Lady Lindsey exclaimed.

"Oh, yes, Lady Lindsey, I heard you quite well, and I thoroughly understand your concern. However, I do not believe we personally are in any danger. That is, at this time."

"Well, honey, what do we do now?" Elizabeth Ann begged.

"Just be as normal as you can. Relax and continue your regular activities. I would, however, suggest that you do not leave the building unless you are accompanied by someone you are very familiar with. Just for safety reasons, of course."

"Well, if you say so..." Lady Lindsey said. "I'll try."

Then Reuben changed the subject. "Lady Lindsey?" he inquired.

"Yes, Reuben?" she replied.

"Is Constance still working on her novel?" he asked subtly.

"Oh, yes," Lady Lindsey proudly responded. "She has had several meetings with several influential persons concerning her writings. Madam MaRooska planned for several authors to consult her and help her finish the last chapters."

"I do hope all goes well," Reuben murmured.

"I detect some skepticism in your remark," Lady Lindsey said.

"Well, I know the last time she was at this resort, she did not finish the last chapters. I am concerned about her mental attitude and health."

All Reuben could think of was what Charles Wolf had told him about the movie rights being stolen right out from under Constance's nose before she even finished the novel.

Then Reuben added, "We all need to be especially careful about getting too familiar with the guests we meet here."

"I firmly agree," Lady Lindsey said.

She was remembering the information that Virginia Camille had gotten from the computer belonging to the Barbados twins. Constance, Virginia Camille, and Lady Lindsey were fully aware that these twins had stolen the rights to her novel, even before she completed the book. But what to do next was the missing piece of this puzzle.

Charles Wolf had been Alisha D'La Chaisson's personal business advisor, and his firm, Wolf and Boudreaux, had handled the D'La Chaisson fortune for decades. Alisha's father and grandfather had both used this firm. Charles Wolf knew everything about the family assets. When Charles discovered the missing accounts, he knew a thorough investigation would be needed to locate the lost documents and accounts – the quicker, the better. When this money changed hands, it took much more time to locate the parties involved and where the money landed. The money may have been moved two or three times into different accounts.

The telephone rang, and Reuben answered. "Hello? Yes, this is he. Yes, I will take the call."

It was Charles. "Charles, I was expecting you to call yesterday. I understand completely."

Reuben listened attentively while Charles gave him the updated details that his private investigator had found.

"Yes, yes, I understand. I will talk to them as soon as I can. Yes, I understand the urgency of this matter. Yes, I understand our lives may be in danger."

Reuben immediately hung up the phone. He looked at his watch. He knew that Virginia Camille and Constance would not be back in the building until dinner was served. Elizabeth Ann was with Lady Lindsey. They had taken the limousine to Londonberry Estates. They would return around 6:00 PM. Reuben knew he had to work fast. He sat down at his computer and began to search the overseas accounts. He used the transaction numbers that Charles Wolf had given him, two code names, to get into the accounts.

He was quickly given access to the computer code. After this, the Singapore and Cayman Islands accounts opened. These two offices had sent their accounts to Zurich, Switzerland, listed as "A.D. 0008". The Cayman and Singapore accounts were wiped clean. Reuben was very shocked to see another window open. The Hollywood studio was linked, along with the name "Alisha D'La Chaisson" from Lafayette, Louisiana.

Then he saw in big bold print: "Angel Doll".

Reuben slowly began to make the connection. There was no way that Lady Lindsey's family assets would have been connected with Alisha D'La Chaisson's family assets unless there was an inside perpetrator who knew both families well enough and would be familiar enough with their financial wealth and their holdings.

Later that afternoon, Constance and Virginia Camille were resting in their rooms.

"What do you think Reuben wants to talk to us about?" Virginia Camille asked.

"I have no idea," Constance answered. "But he did say it was urgent."

Then there was a knock on the door. Constance went to the door and opened it.

"Well, hello, Inspector Barnes and Inspector Gibbs. What can we do for you all?"

"Just routine questioning," Inspector Barnes replied. "We would like to ask you a few more questions."

"Fine," Virginia Camille answered. "Won't you gentlemen sit down?"

"Thank you," Inspector Gibbs said. They both took a seat on the chairs.

"I guess you have heard by now the body that was found was that of Countess Christina Andrews from Scotland?" inquired Inspector Barnes.

"Yes," Constance sighed. "We heard that this morning. It is so sad. Who would want to kill such a lovely person? She was killed sometime on Tuesday night. The coroner's lab pinpointed the death to be in the early morning hours, two days ago."

Then Inspector Barnes said, "From my investigation, I have concluded that all guests of Madam MaRooska's Specialty Resort were in the building Tuesday night."

Virginia Camille looked at the inspector. She knew Ralph's brother was not in the building. Now, where he was, no one knew, but Ralph had covered for his brother, saying he was in the building.

"If you girls hear anything suspicious," the inspector said. "Please let us know."

"We will." Constance opened the door and let the men out.

Virginia Camille was still very suspicious. She knew these men were dangerous, and she did not put it past them to be involved in the murder scheme. She had not quite figured out the "why" yet.

When 6:30 rolled around, Reuben called and told Virginia Camille, Constance, and Lady Lindsey to meet at the library. They had an especially important issue to discuss. Arriving at the library, they saw Reuben and Elizabeth Ann were sitting in a corner, facing an outside window that overlooked the tennis courts. Reuben stood up and motioned for them to come to him.

Virginia Camille was the first to speak up. "This had better be important. I had to break a date."

"It is important," Reuben declared. "It is very important."

The ladies sat down at the table. Reuben had copied several documents from his computer to show the dilemma of the family fortunes. He handed each lady a stapled copy of the information he was going to discuss. As the group began to assemble at the table, the William and Mary grandfather clock's secret peephole opened. The revolving eye turned toward the conversation in the corner.

"What's this all about?" Lady Lindsey asked.

"It is basically an extortion scheme," Reuben replied.

"What are you talking about?" questioned Virginia Camille.

"Charles Wolf has been investigating our family assets and online accounts. He has found illegal activities taking place over the past six months. The D'La Chaisson family inheritance is in jeopardy. We are missing over twenty-two million dollars, and Charles is using a private investigator to locate the money. Lady Lindsey, your wealth is also in jeopardy. Various overseas accounts of yours have been compromised. Lady Lindsey, they have not been misplaced. They have been stolen. Charles is fairly sure that a person here at Madam MaRooska's is a third party to the scam."

"I knew it, I knew it!" Virginia Camille screamed. "My suspicions must be accurate. When that angel doll showed up in that orchid rose box, I knew I had not dreamed it up."

"Angel doll?" Constance asked. "What has an angel doll got to do with this situation?"

"The money has been sent to a Swiss bank account in Zurich, Switzerland. The accounts are labeled 'AD 0008'. AD stands for 'Angel Doll.'"

"Then there is a connection between my Angel Doll novel and the one at the studio in Hollywood," Constance stated.

"Yes," Reuben answered. "The movie rights have been stolen, and your name is no longer connected to the book, finished or unfinished. But that is not the worst part. Our lives are in danger." He gulped.

"What do you mean, 'in danger'?" Lady Lindsey asked.

"I mean you could be killed if we attempt to cross the criminals. These men or women are smart and corrupt people. They know all about our family and our lives back home in the states. Charles warned me that we had better be careful in dealing with them. They have killed before and will not hesitate to kill again."

"So, what do we do now?" Constance asked.

Reuben continued. "Charles Wolf has told me that tomorrow afternoon, the private investigator will be here in Ireland. They will be disguised as horse owners and trainers. They will be staying at a hotel near Londonberry Estates. All of us will be under their protection.

Cooperate fully with them because they are very much aware of this corrupt scam and how it is supposed to play out. The men are here to protect us."

"This makes my literally sick," Constance said, and then she began to hyperventilate. "I am sick and need to go back to the room."

"We need to get her back to the room to rest," Lady Lindsey stated. "This scare is too much for her. The angel doll experience is beginning to take its toll again. We must get her to the room."

Then Virginia Camille stated, "Do not call a doctor. These men are dangerous. I feel I know enough about the situation, and we must handle it ourselves."

"You are right," Reuben stammered. "The investigators will be here, and they will inform us of what to do. Go back to your rooms. Do not answer any phone calls. Stay in your rooms tomorrow, no matter what is going on. When Mr. Wolf and the investigators arrive, I will send for you all. We can meet in my room. Am I making myself clear?"

The ladies shook their heads in disbelief and horror. They left the library and went to their designated rooms for the night.

The next day, Reuben was contacted by the private investigator who was hired by Charles Wolf.

Rueben told Elizabeth Anne, "Honey, call Constance, Lady Lindsey, and Virginia Camille. Tell them to meet us outside the building in thirty minutes."

"Okay, dear," Elizabeth Anne responded.

Thirty minutes later, Reuben and four ladies boarded one of the estate's limousines and headed for Bishop Gates Hotel, which was outside Londonberry Estates. The ride was incredibly quiet. Reuben had instructed the ladies not to breathe a word while riding in the limo. This was a very delicate matter, and secrecy was of prime importance. The ride took well over forty minutes. There was a lot of traffic on the road. So many competitors and guests had already begun to arrive for the horse racing event.

The limo driver made an announcement: "Bishop Gate Hotel, arriving in five minutes."

The four ladies got out of the limousine and Reuben tipped the driver.

Arriving at the main office, Reuben made his way to the front desk and began talking to the desk clerk. He asked for the room of Alfred Buckley. The clerk directed them to room 407. It was seven doors to the right of the elevator. Reuben knocked on the door, and a tall gentleman opened it and directed the five guests to come in.

"I'm Alfred Buckley, and this is Windsor Ratley."

The men were dressed in awfully expensive attire. Then Mr. Buckley explained their cover identities. "We are joint owners of Simply Majestic. Our horse will be racing in the event tomorrow. We understand that Charles Wolf is paying us to ensure your protection while you are here in Ireland."

"Yes," Reuben answered. "Did he explain everything to you of our circumstances?"

"Quite thoroughly," Mr. Ratley replied.

Then Mr. Buckley suggested, "Why don't you all sit down while I make us some tea?"

The ladies took their seats on the long leather sofa, and Reuben sat in a tall wingback chair.

"Mr. D'La Chaisson," Mr. Buckley said. "We cannot tell you everything we know about this investigation. However, we can disclose some of the measures we have in place to ensure the safety of you and your families and your finances."

Then Mr. Ratley added, "Eighty percent of your family wealth has been confiscated. The money has been moved several times to different bank accounts. Alisha D'La Chaisson's accounts went first, followed by all your property and withholdings – from Bastrop, Louisiana, to the East Coast. Perhaps the biggest surprise of all is the largest film industry in Hollywood is in a worldwide lawsuit for stealing the copyrights of certain books. They have changed the author's names and maneuvered the royalties to unauthorized authors. Miss Constance Stallings' unfinished novel, The Angel Doll, was stolen three years ago. The perpetrators conspired with this Hollywood film company. They obtained the movie rights to her book, and a large amount of money was put in a Swiss account."

"Who was the third party?" Lady Lindsey asked. "There is no way this confidential information and knowledge could leak out unless the third party knew all of our family really well."

"That is precisely what we believe," Alfred Buckley said. "However, the third-party person must have known all the details when Miss Stallings was here three years ago. I do not believe the Barbados twins and the third party are both working for the same organization, but they use the same code names and the same bank accounts. Scotland Yard suspects that the mysterious murder of the maid three years ago was a part of this organization."

As the men talked, Constance began to look sicker. This brought back terrible memories of her first visit to Bellingfast Estates.

At this time, Reuben interjected. "So, you fellows believe that this extortion scam could be part of a bigger conspiracy?"

"Precisely," the investigator answered, "We need to warn you all that these people are corrupt. They have dealings in drugs and gambling. The big money comes from being in this criminal organization."

Virginia Camille let out a bewildered breath and said, "Many of these people at this resort are the wealthiest persons from around the globe. They are here for a two-week stay. We do not know how many or which guests are engaged in criminal activities."

"That is why, Miss Virginia Camille Stallings," Alfred Buckley replied. "None of the murders are ever solved, and the money laundering goes undetected. Nothing is ever solved when it happens at Bellingfast Estates events."

The ladies all looked at each other with mixed feelings of fear and awe. They were terrified at being involved in a extortion scam. Leaving The Bishop's Gate Hotel,

Reuben instructed the ladies to not mention a word of what had been discussed that day in the hotel room. The limousine traveled back to Bellingfast Estates.

Chapter 10

The Grand National Horse Race

Under the strain of the murder investigation, there was a great deal of commotion and confusion at Bellingfast Estates. The guests were very apprehensive, just wondering who the next victim would be. However, in the neighboring castle at Londonberry Estates, the staff was very actively preparing for the upcoming horse race. Horse owners and trainers were coming in from all parts of the world. Londonberry was completely booked, and neighboring lodges and hotels were filling up fast. The Londonberry stables were buzzing with activity. Trainers, owners, and business executives were very engaged with all the activities. All the entries had arrived for the main event. There were horses, which were scheduled to compete. As quick as the horses arrived, the bets began coming in. The betting office was quite busy. They were opening at 6:30 AM and closing as late as 9:00 PM.

Lord Tutwiller was quite visible in the betting arena. The trainers, breeders, owners, and jockeys were very much aware of the importance of the industry. It was crucial for the owners to supervise the elite group in the betting office to ensure fairness. Each owner had at least five or six persons hired as undercover agents to be sure nothing illegal took place. Even under the best of circumstances, many corrupt activities did take place. Each owner needed to protect and ensure the safety of his horse and his jockeys. The horses were monitored twenty-four hours a day. The stakes were so high, and one could not risk an accident, either one of happenstance or deliberate tampering.

Two days before the event began, all jockeys and horses were weighed to ensure the proper accountability for the upcoming race. Lord Tutwiller hired his own investigating committee to be sure no fraudulent activity would be going on before and during the races. All competitors had to be screened prior to the race and the results to be sent to the screening committee for evaluation. From the thorough investigation, the prospects for the upcoming race were good. It showed that no criminal corruptness was evident. As a result, all races would begin as scheduled.

For the past year, competitions for this final annual event had been going on all over England and Ireland. Several hundred horse racing events had taken place to finalize and eliminate horses. Only the best would compete for the Grand National at Londonberry Estates. Lord Tutwiller had hosted this main event for the last twenty years. He had met many influential people from all parts of Europe. He had developed many close friendships over the years.

These were the fifteen final horses listed in alphabetical order:

BLUSHING JOHN
CHAMPION HURDLE
DOUBLE CHANCE
HEDGEHUNTER
HURRICANE FLY
IRISH OPEN
MOSCONE BALLET
PRINCESS PATE
RACHEL ALEXANDER
RED RUN
SIMPLY MAJESTIC
SON OF BRIARTIC
STAFF OF WRITER
STRIKE GOLD
WINDSOR SLIPPER

The horse racing events at Londonberry Estates were well underway. The participants had officially signed in, and each horse had qualified. The Londonberry Festival and racing events were the most prestigious and glamorous of the twenty-five race courses in Ireland. These events dated back to 1868. This national event would last for five days. The spectator stands had been freshly painted. There were two separate stands adjacent to each other. Each stand was full, and hundreds of people were lined up inside the fence. They were just hoping to get a glance as the races began. The larger stand was three decks high. There were rows and rows of spectator seats in each stand. The spectator seats were perfect to see the event. There was a row of glass boxes to view the race. These seats were awfully expensive because when sitting in these seats, attendees could stay dry. They were sold to elite visitors. The other stand was in a semi-circle. It was covered with a top. It would hold about two thousand spectators.

The horses and the riders were lined up for the entry parade. As the horses rode by, they were inspected. They were given a chance to warm up on the grassy trail. All bets were in, and the fifteen horses were at the starting barrier. An electric machine was used to ensure a fair start. The gates blocked the horses into their narrow stalls. The Londonberry Cup awarded at the end of this race had over five million wagers each year. Therefore, horse racing was very lucrative for Ireland's economy.

The spectator stands were all full. The glass boxes were full to the brim. Everyone wanted to get the best view. Crowds and crowds of people were standing outside the arena. The estimates for the week exceeded one hundred thousand persons in attendance.

As the trainers and horses made their final parade toward the starting gate, the crowds began to cheer with enthusiasm. Truly, this day was full of excitement for all of Ireland. Everyone was watching the clock. The race was to begin at 4:00 PM. The horses were to run a two-mile course in this race. As the horses lined up at the starting gate, the crowd began to quiet. They watched attentively as the moment was about to begin.

The gun went off, and the race began.

The horses had to make five laps around the arena to complete the two-mile course.

After the first lap, Simply Majestic is in the lead. Strike Gold and Hudgehunter were neck and neck for second and third place. Several yards back was Irish Open, and behind him was Red Run. The remainder of the horses were scattered behind on the race track. The crowds were standing and using their binoculars. They were looking down from their glass boxes, wondering who would be leading in the second lap. As they round to the second lap, Simply Majestic was still in the lead. Hedgehunter was in second, and Simply Gold was in third. Irish Open and Princess Pate were close at fourth and fifth. Red Run was in the sixth spot.

As the race horses continued to race around the track for the third lap, Hedgehunter took the lead. Simply Majestic was now in second place. Irish Open, Princess Pate, and Red Run were all steady at third, fourth, and fifth places. Trailing in sixth place was Double Chance. There were only two more laps in the race. As the fourth lap began, Hedgehunter was still in a slight lead, with Simply Majestic and Irish Open right behind him. Double Chance and Blushing John were next in the race, followed by Princess Pate and Red Run.

It looked like Hedgehunter would be the winner.

As the second half of the fifth lap came, Irish Open took off. He passed Simply Majestic and Hedgehunter. The crowds were screaming. Irish Open had surprised everyone. He took a leap of energy and was now leading the race.

As the crowds yelled, it was obvious that Irish Open would be the winner.

The crowds were standing and cheering. This had been a very commendable event. Irish Open was predicted to come in third, and now he had made an about-face. He has taken the first position by leaps and bounds. The crowd had mixed emotions. Thousands of people had put their wagers on Simply Majestic. Simply Majestic had been predicted to win from the beginning of the race. Major businesses and government officials had also wagered on Simply Majestic. There also was a lot of money bet on Hedgehunter. There were a lot of disappointed investors. They would be going home empty-handed while, on the other hand, all those who bet on Irish Open were thrilled with the outcome of the race.

As Irish Open, his jockey, and the owners went down for final pictures, the rest of the crowds watched with anticipation. Garland and roses were put around the horse's neck. The crowds went under the stands to collect the money they had won. Irish Open had made a lot of investors incredibly happy. Within hours, most of the crowds were dispersed. All the owners and trainers, along with the horses, were making their way out of Londonberry Estates. Lord Tutwiller was busy talking with all the guests. He was encouraging all of them to make plans to come back the next year.

Madam MaRooska, Lady Lindsey, Constance, and Virginia Camille had all ridden together.

As they were making their way toward the limo, Lord Tutwiller motioned to Lady Lindsey. "I'll be over Friday. We have a lot of things to discuss." Then he said to Madam MaRooska, "Tell William Jeffery to have our horses ready for us to go on a ride after lunch."

As he returned to his guest, Lady Lindsey remarked, "I wonder what he wants to discuss with me."

"He simply likes you," Constance remarked.

"Just like we all do," Madam MaRooska replied.

Then the four ladies boarded their limo and headed for Bellingfast Estates.

Friday morning, Lady Lindsey was called to the main hall. She had a guest, and she figured it was Lord Tutwiller.

He walked to meet her and said, "Let us go to the study. I presume it will be more private."

Lady Lindsey had no idea what was up, but so many strange events had transpired, anything was possible. When they arrived in the study, no one else was in there. Lady Lindsey knew something was wrong, but she didn't know what it was. She also did not know how the visit was connected to Londonberry Estates.

Lord Tutwiller started the conversation. "Scotland Yard's commissioner came to see me two days before the races began. I had so much on my mind with the upcoming race that I did not say anything to anyone. They were inquiring about the murder of Countess Christina

Anderson."

"Have they found the murderer?" Lady Lindsey asked.

"No," he responded. "But they have some mighty good leads as to who committed this horrendous act. Anyway, that's not why I am here today. I am here to question you about the angel doll that was in Constance's story."

Lady Lindsey shrieked and then asked, "Why are you bringing the angel doll up? Why are you even bringing Constance's novel up at all?"

Lady Lindsey remembered the meeting at The Bishop Gates Hotel when Alfred Buckley, the private investigator for Charles Wolf, specifically instructed them not to mention a word about his visit.

When Lord Tutwiller did not respond, she gave her best explanation. "Well, we don't know anything about the death of the countess. I came to Bellingfast with my nieces, Constance and Virginia Camille. Constance was supposed to finish her novel. That is all I know about this matter."

Lord Tutwiller began to dig deeper. "Then there is your nephew and his wife, Elizabeth Ann D'La Chaisson. When and why did the decide to join you on this trip?"

Lady Lindsey was appalled. By now, she was very suspicious.

She thought to herself, Why is he so interested my family?

She decided it was best if she simply dropped the conversation.

"Did you come over for us to ride?" Lady Lindsey inquired.

"Oh, yes," he replied. "William Jeffery told Madam MaRooska that the horses are ready, so we can go."

Immediately, Lady Lindsey and Lord Tutwiller headed toward the stables. The horses were ready. A stable hand brought the horses out, and Lord Tutwiller and Lady Lindsey proceeded to go to the trails.

"I think we will go on the Lake Forest trail near the Mountain Brook by the old cave," Lord Tutwiller suggested.

Lady Lindsey did not think anything about it until Lord Tutwiller mentioned. "This is the same trail that Constance and the countess were on when the storm occurred."

Lady Lindsey looked frightened.

She thought, Why would he be taking the same route on which the disaster occurred?

She continued to ride, but the more she rode, the more frightened she became. Lady Lindsey's strong trust in Lord Tutwiller was diminishing. As they traveled on, Lord Tutwiller recognized the place at which they had arrived.

"Lady Lindsey," Lord Tutwiller remarked. "This is the cave that Constance and Countess Christina spent the night during the terrible storm."

"I want to go back to the resort," Lady Lindsey said, admitting, "I am scared."

"No," Lord Tutwiller stated firmly. "You must know all the facts before we return."

"What are you talking about?" she questioned.

"Come on in and follow me," Lord Tutwiller demanded.

Lord Tutwiller got off his horse and helped Lady Lindsey get off her horse. They proceeded inside the cave. The cave was very dark, and Lord Tutwiller used his lantern. He pointed to a certain spot and showed it to Lady Lindsey.

"This is where Countess Christina's body was found."

"Why are you telling me this?!" Lady Lindsey screamed.

"Because, Lady Lindsey," he abruptly answered. "The countess was not the intended victim. Constance was the one who was intended to be murdered."

Lady Lindsey nearly fainted.

Lord Tutwiller continued to explain, saying, "The Scotland Yard commissioners have the Barbados twins in custody. The men have not admitted to anything. However, the detectives confiscated their computers and telephones. They ran background checks on these men. They both are connected with organized crime. They are working out of the greater New Orleans, Louisiana area. Lady Lindsey, their computers have details of business transactions of yours and Reuben's mother, Alisha Christina D'La Chaisson. The money has been transferred to offshore bank accounts."

After these explanations, Lady Lindsey was very puzzled. She asked, "Why would these people want to murder my niece?"

"Constance's unfinished book, The Angel Doll, has already been published," Lord Tutwiller explained. "But the title has been changed. It is on the bestseller list with no mention of Constance's name. This organization has stolen the book rights from her. It was the intention to have her murdered while she is at Bellingfast, but wires got crossed, and the wrong person was killed."

"So, what do we do now?" Lady Lindsey asked.

"I'm working with Scotland Yards to solve the mystery. We are up to that point. We have no concrete evidence to indict these two men. You cannot indict someone for murder just because they have confiscated a lot of business transactions and added them to another account. The commissioners believe there is a third party involved with this leakage of information. The third party is coming out of Baton Rouge, Louisiana business holdings."

Lady Lindsey felt it was extremely important not to say anything about Charles Wolf or Alfred Buckley, especially at this time.

"Let's get on back to Bellingfast," Lord Tutwiller recommended.

The two got on the horses and headed back to the resort.

Chapter 11

Private Business Matters

Gladys and Gertrude were in the kitchen cleaning up after a banquet. They were alone, so they could talk.

"The last time you looked, how many dolls were left in that crate?" Gertrude asked Gladys.

"I think there were four or five. I never really counted. I never had any reason to be so careful or cautious. I think we have sold ten or fifteen of the dolls."

"The money has been safely stored in the pantry safe," Gertrude answered. "I check the money every few days, and it is all there."

"Good," Gladys said, but she was still puzzled. "Do you think the dolls could connect us with the countess's murder?"

"Of course not," Gertrude quickly responded. "Do not even concern yourself with that thought. There is no connection at all. Nobody knows anything."

Truthfully, both women wondered what had happened to the remaining dolls.

Gertrude thought to herself, I am going back to the wine cellar and look for myself.

Maybe, just maybe, Gladys overlooked the dolls, or maybe she overlooked them at the last count. When Gertrude got through talking, the tall turquoise clock on the kitchen countertop made a slight noise, as a peephole revolved back into the regular position. Yes, someone had been watching Gladys and Gertrude as they discussed the missing angel dolls. But why all the secrecy and mischief?

Nobody knew about the dolls except Gertrude and Gladys... or so they thought.

Miss Hatfield's mother was incredibly familiar with the woman who was murdered at Londonberry Estates. The woman told Miss Hatfield's mother about the angel doll and how she had stolen it. Most of the Negroes believed the story to be true. The news got out about the murder and how Christina's autopsy indicated that she was Caucasian. That was enough. Miss Hatfield knew that a replica copy of the angel doll could bring lots of money for those who believed the Negro legend. That was when she decided to make the move to Bellingfast Estates. She and Gertrude formed a successful business making and selling the replica dolls.

Later that night, after everyone had gone to bed, Gertrude put her robe on and sneaked out of her room. She headed down toward the wine cellar to see for herself.

After rummaging through all the boxes, it was apparent to her that the dolls were not in the wine cellar.

So where were they?

I'd better go check the pantry safe, Gertrude thought. Just to be sure the money is still there.

She quietly left the wine cellar and headed to the pantry closet. Inside the pantry closet was the safe. She quickly used the combination to open it and discovered the twenty thousand Swiss Francs were gone. Frightened, she looked again to be sure her eyes had not failed her. She was shocked and frightened.

To Gertrude's knowledge, only she and Gladys were involved in this scheme. Nobody else knew about the dolls or the buyers. Now, Gertrude was worried. This illegal business of selling the angel dolls could affect her employment at Bellingfast. But worse yet, the police could possibly try to connect Gladys and Gertrude to the murder of Countess Christina. Gertrude quickly rushed out of the pantry. When she tried to open the kitchen door, it was locked. It was 3:30 AM, and someone locked her in the kitchen. All she could do was wait on Gladys. Gladys usually arrived to work at 5:30 AM. Gertrude just sat in a chair until Gladys arrived.

At 5:15 AM, Gladys arrived and used her key to open the kitchen door. When she saw Gertrude sleeping in the chair, she was startled.

"What are you doing in here, Gertrude?" Gladys stammered.

Gertrude began to wake up to explain the situation. "I came down to the kitchen last night. I wanted to check in the kitchen pantry safe to be sure the money was still there. Gladys, the money is gone."

"What?!" Gladys hollered back. "What do you mean?"

"Go look for yourself," Gertrude instructed her. "Go look for yourself."

Then Gladys and Gertrude walked through the kitchen to the pantry. Gladys used the combination to open the safe. Sure enough, the money was gone.

"Who took it?!" Gladys snapped.

"I do not know! Nobody ever uses the safe, except you or me. I do not know if anybody else even knows the combination."

"What about Sissily?" Gladys interjected.

"She never comes into the pantry. I always have the staple foods and ingredients ready for her on the kitchen counter," Gertrude explained.

"Why were you sleeping in the chair when I came in?" Gladys questioned her again.

"Because I could not open the kitchen door to my room," Gertrude admitted. "Some way or another, when I tried to leave the kitchen, the door was locked."

"So, what did you do?" Gladys inquired.

"I just went to sleep and decided to wait on you. That is all I could do," Gertrude answered.

"Well, we had better get busy preparing breakfast," Gladys reminded Gertrude. "The guests will be in at 7:00 AM to 7:30 AM, so we had better get started."

The kitchen door swung open.

"Good morning, ladies," Sissily greeted them in a cheerful manner. "You look awful, Gertrude. Did you not sleep well last night?"

"I did not sleep well at all last night."

"Well," Sissily said. "Why don't you take it easy? Gladys and I can get this breakfast ready."

"Well, alright," Gertrude agreed. "I'm going to my room. I'm going to wash my face. Maybe I will feel better."

As Gertrude left the kitchen, she still wondered about her lost key.

When she opened the door to her room, she saw her key.

It was on the cedar chest. Gertrude was very confused. All she could figure was that the kitchen door was not locked, and she just thought it was. Then she tried to figure out the reason that she could not open it from inside.

Oh well, she thought.

Gertrude was much too frustrated for one night. She went into the bathroom to make herself presentable for the day's work.

Later on that day, Reuben told Elizabeth Ann to call Lady Lindsey and tell her to have the group meet on the top wing in the conservatory at 6:00 PM.

"Have you heard anything, dear?" Elizabeth asked.

"Yes, Inspector Alfred Buckley called me this morning. He has some new information regarding the stolen transactions from the Singapore and Cayman Island accounts. The twenty million dollars has been accounted for, and they are in the process of sending the money back to the states. However, a third co-conspirator has not been identified."

At 6:00 PM the next afternoon, Reuben had planned a meeting with Constance, Lady Lindsey and Virginia Camille in the top wing in the observatory. He was going to share the new information that he had learned from Charles Wolf and private investigator, Alfred Buckley.

"Are we safe yet?" Lady Lindsey asked. "Are we being protected?"

"Yes and no," Reuben tried to explain. "Alfred Buckley knew Scotland Yard had confiscated the Barbados twins' computer. All the money that the men transferred to the Singapore office and the Cayman Island office has been found."

"Where is it?" Constance asked. "It has been put into a Swiss bank account," Reuben explained. "It seems like there is an open account in Zurich, Switzerland, which added twenty million dollars from the Angel Doll money."

"What does that mean?" Constance questioned.

"Just as we suspected," Reuben answered. "Somebody stole the movie rights to your book."

Quickly, Lady Lindsey spoke up. "And someone wants Constance dead."

The whole group looked shocked as they stared at Lady Lindsey.

"Lord Tutwiller works with Scotland Yard," she explained. "And the murder of the countess was a mistake. Lord Tutwiller and Scotland Yard feel absolutely sure that Constance was the intended victim."

The expressions of everyone in the group clearly conveyed the question "why?".

Lady Lindsey continued, "Because of the Angel Doll account and the twenty million dollars that was put in the account. The Hollywood studio had to verify this information. With Constance dead, nobody would ever know who the real author was, and twenty million dollars would lie waiting for the writer to pick up the dividends."

"So, as we asked..." Reuben interrupted. "What do we do now?"

Constance spoke up first. "I suggest we all take the next plane back to Baton Rouge. I am really scared for my life."

As Constance was talking, the mantle clock that was sitting on an Edwardian mahogany chest began to open and close on the right side next to a Roman numeral. It was quite apparent that the five of them were being watched and, perhaps, recorded.

Early the next morning, Scotland Yard made an unexpected visit to Madam MaRooska's Specialty Resort. Sir Callahan greeted the men. The commissioner and the deputy commissioner made the urgent request to talk to Madam MaRooska immediately, and Sir Callahan used his intercom to call her. Sir Callahan informed the commissioners that she would meet with them in her private office and led them there.

"Well," Madam MaRooska said. "What brings you men here this early in the morning? Is there any new information on the case?"

Sir Basil Thomson, the commissioner, spoke up first. "Madam MaRooska, we know your guests are to depart to their homes in two days."

"However," Deputy Commissioner Sir Bernard Hogan quickly interjected. "Madam MaRooska, we are about to solve this murder, and we cannot allow any of your guests to leave the premises."

"What?!" Madam MaRooska shrieked in astonishment. "What are you talking about?"

"We are coming close to solving this murder, and we cannot take any chances. Therefore, we cannot allow any guests to leave."

"So what do I tell them?" Madam MaRooska asked. "This is very unprofessional and embarrassing. I cannot understand all of this."

"Do not allow any of the guests to leave," the commissioner snapped. "Hopefully, this will only be a delay of three or four days."

"Well, I certainly hope so," Madam MaRooska huffed. "This is preposterous. I am very disgusted and embarrassed to tears. I will make an announcement tonight to warn the guests of the delay. I'll call Sir Callahan, and he can see you all out."

The whole resort was buzzing with excitement. News had spread quickly about the visit from Scotland Yard. All the guests were overly concerned. They all wanted to know why Madam MaRooska had called a meeting in the dining hall in the evening.

Throughout the day, the guests scurried about, trying to figure out and understand what this unexpected meeting was all about. The Barbados twins had been released from Scotland Yard because the evidence was insufficient to prove they were involved with the death of the countess. As the twins were sitting in their room, a message popped up on their computer.

The message read:

TAKE THE FIRST FLIGHT OUT OF BELFAST. USE THE BELFAST CITY AIRPORT. TAKE CAUTION AND DO NOT FLY INTO DUBLIN. IT IS TOO DANGEROUS. MAKE IMMEDIATE PLANS TO LEAVE. DO NOT WORRY ABOUT YOUR LUGGAGE. JUST BRING YOUR BUSINESS PAPERS AND YOUR COMPUTERS. ALL OTHER INFORMATION WILL BE PROVIDED FOR YOU.

"Well," Sir Reggie Renaldo said. "What could all of this be about?"

"I have no idea," Sir Ralph Grantly responded. "But we had best get started."

As they were quickly preparing to leave, an announcement came over the intercom. The message asked all to stop what they were doing and listen.

"This is Basil Thomson, the commissioner from Scotland Yard. I have an important announcement. All the guests here at Bellingfast Estates need to be aware of the significance of what I am about to say. You may not leave the building. We have Scotland Yard policemen posted at all the doors leading out. You will be arrested and taken into custody if you try to leave the building. Again, it is imperative that you do not try to leave the building. I understand that Madam MaRooska will be meeting with you tonight to discuss this matter. She will be giving you further details. There is no other way to solve this mysterious murder. Thank you for your cooperation."

Chapter 12

The Barbados Twins Make Their Escape

The Barbados twins hurried toward the side entrance. Hopefully, the Metropolitan police had not arrived. Leaving through the unprotected side door, Sir Adams flagged the black limousine. He and Sir Reggie quickly got into the limo. They demanded the driver take them to the Belfast Airport and make it as fast as possible. Upon arriving at the airport, an aircraft was waiting for them with its pilot at the ready. They climbed up the steps and got into the airplane.

Within five minutes, the Cessna Citation Mustang was in the air. It was heading for Argentina. At 8:00 PM sharp, the meeting was held in the banquet hall. Madam MaRooska stood up and got the attention of the guests. She began to make the announcements that Scotland Yard had directed.

She began, saying, "I am very despondent to have to bring you this news. Commissioner Sir Basil Thomson and Deputy Commissioner Menzies have instructed us to close the doors of Bellingfast for the next four or five days. You cannot leave the building. Your airline flights will have to be cancelled until further notice. The murder of the countess is still under investigation. Her husband is flying in tomorrow. He will be working with Scotland Yard to solve the murder."

Several guests began to speak up.

"Madam MaRooska, Madam MaRooska!"

"I must leave Ireland," the governor from Arizona demanded. "I cannot wait three more days. I have important business back in the United States."

Then Dr. Wellington stood up. "This is preposterous. The police cannot hold us here. I have got business meetings. I have executives flying in for a regional meeting. They cannot hold us here."

Edward Harper agreed. "I am a stockbroker from Australia, and I must be back by the first of next week. I cannot believe this nonsense."

Reuben looked at Lady Lindsey, and he nodded like it was going to be okay.

"What do you think?" Lady Lindsey asked.

"I do believe it would be advisable for our party to stay at least another week."

"Oh, no..." Constance was hyperventilating.

"Constance, calm down, calm down," Reuben said to her sternly. "We are not going to be able to solve this back in Louisiana. I do believe that some of the questions and answers about the murder will still be brought to light."

Virginia Camille looked around for the Barbados twins. "I knew it, I knew it! The boys from Barbados are gone! I saw them early this morning, and I figured they would try to make a quick departure. I knew they were in jail for suspicion of murder, and sure enough they are gone."

Elizabeth Ann was tugging on Reuben's sleeve. "Honey, what do we do now? I am scared. What do we do now?" She was pestering him with alarming questions.

As the guests were dispersing from the dining hall, it was obvious that all the guests were angry and upset. These guests at the resort all led a terribly busy life. Each person had plans for the following week. Now everything was up in the air.

Nine hours later, the Cessna Citation Mustang was circling the Buenos Aires, Argentina airport. There were only two passengers on the plane with the pilot and co-pilot. Upon landing, a limo with a chauffeur approached the men. Sir Ralph Grantley Adams and Sir Reggie Renaldo Adams knew the limousine was for them. After they boarded the limo, the driver headed for the elite hotel, The Alvcar Palace in Buenos Aires. This hotel was one of the most luxurious hotels around the world. As the limo arrived at the hotel, one of the dedicated staff greeted the two men and escorted them to the Embassy Suite on the top floor. As the elevator opened into the elegant room, Caesar Augustus Rodney, an ambassador from Argentina, walked toward them and gave each a warm embrace.

"So glad you men were able to get away," he said. "I realize that the Scotland Yard police put Bellingfast Estates under surveillance. They are not allowing anyone to leave for the next week."

"Yes, we were lucky to get out," Sir Ralph replied. "The police had not reported for duty, so we were able to slip away."

"Please come in. Would you like a drink?"

"Gin and tonic," Sir Reggie requested.

"Same for me," Sir Ralph stated.

"I've talked with your uncle, Ambassador Leon Palmer. He is very displeased with the situation at Bellingfast. This is a stressful situation. It has caused a lot of unnecessary pain and anxiety. Plus, the unsurmountable dividends have been squandered on miscalculations."

"But, Ambassador, we did what we were told to do," Sir Ralph tried to explain.

"Yes, Ambassador, we arrived at Bellingfast," Sir Reggie added. "And the instructions that were given to us were followed specifically."

"Not specific enough," the Ambassador shouted. "You murdered the wrong person."

"What? Why?" Both Sir Reggie and Sir Ralph screamed in astonishment.

"You must be kidding. You are mistaken."

"No, gentlemen, you are mistaken. I'll repeat it: you murdered the wrong person. You have put us in financial strain. When your personal computers were confiscated by Scotland Yard, they were able to unlock all our accounts. The police have uncovered all of the personal files from the Singapore office, and the Cayman Island accounts have been closed permanently."

"What about the money in the Zurich negotiations?" Sir Reggie asked.

"Well, the studio is terribly upset. They have wired us several times asking about the death of Constance Stallings."

"What did you tell them?" Sir Reggie asked.

"What else could we say?" the ambassador from Argentina exclaimed in a disgusted manner. "What could we tell them?"

The Barbados twins were very puzzled. They could not believe that Constance Stallings was to be the murder victim. All the confiscated computers had identified Christina Langley Andrews as the author of The Angel Doll. There was no doubt about it. Someone had tampered with the basic information being transferred from joint bank accounts to the destination at the Zurich bank.

"Your uncle sent specific instructions. Don't go back to the United Kingdom. They now are blaming you for the death of the countess."

"But we did not do it," Sir Reggie tried to explain to clear himself.

"It doesn't matter what you say. Scotland Yard is blaming the both of you for this horrendous murder."

"Well, they had us in jail for several days," Sir Reggie explained. "Then they let us go."

"Yes, they had no concrete proof," Sir Ralph added.

"Well, they now have concrete evidence and proof that you two committed the murder of the countess."

Sir Reggie and Sir Ralph looked at each other. They knew that they had not committed this murder. This caused them to wonder where this evidence came from.

"How well do you all know Earl Andrews?" the ambassador asked the men.

Both men hesitated.

"Well, come on and answer me," the ambassador demanded. "Answer my question."

"Well, in the past, we have done some work for the earl of Scotland," Sir Ralph tried to explain. "Just small jobs. They were simple matters that he did not want to handle."

"But we haven't talked with him for over seven or eight months," Sir Reggie added.

"The earl of Scotland swears that you two were being paid a tremendous amount of money to murder his wife."

"That's a damn lie," Sir Ralph swore. "Yes, the arl did proposition us to murder his wife, but we flat refused."

"This is enough for today. Go back down to the front desk and get your room assignment and the key. Do not make any plans to leave your room. Room service will deliver your dinner. Again, do not leave the room and do not make any phone calls from your room. Do you men understand me? Do you understand me?"

"Yes, sir, completely," Sir Reggie responded. "We will not leave the room."

When the twins left the ambassador's room, they were somewhat puzzled by what he had accused them of doing. Upon arriving in their designated room, they were both quite distressed and angry.

"What do you think the is all about?" Sir Reggie asked, trying to understand the situation.

"Beats me," his brother responded. "But one thing is for sure, I do not want to be blamed and convicted for a murder that I did not do. I was willing to be part of an extortion scam, but I really had reservations about killing anyone."

Sir Reggie was panic-stricken.

He reminded his brother, "You know that Uncle Leon will be furious with us."

"I really don't care," Sir Ralph snarled back. "We spent all those months in San Quentin, not him. While we were serving time in San Quentin is when we met Stretch Ratley."

"Oh, yes, I remember," Sir Reggie stated. "Stretch has a brother who's from the New Orleans area. His brother was a private investigator who worked for the law firm that handled the D'La Chaisson's account."

"Yeah, if you remember, after talking with Stretch, we realized that we could easily transfer funds from their account to our account with no murder involvement," said Sir Ralph. "Besides, transferring funds is a lot safer than disposing of a body."

"I have to give Stretch Ratley credit," Sir Reggie interjected. "His brother, Windsor Ratley, was a private investigator, so his information was accurate."

"Well?!" Ralph emphatically snapped. "How did we end up in San Quentin with no money?"

"I don't know, but I knew it would not be safe for us to go back to the Ukraine!" Sir Reggie reminded his brother. "I guess when we get back to Barbados, Uncle Leon will explain everything."

Later that night, the ambassador from Barbados made a call to the ambassador of Argentina.

"Did the boys arrive?" Ambassador Leon Palmer asked.

"Yes, they got here about three hours ago. They are in their room, and I have a private detective watching them to be sure they do not leave."

"Good, I cannot chance any more discrepancies on this matter. The investments have changed hands several times. We must cover tracks for each move that is made. The money is finally safe. The Cayman office was able to clear up the money from Baton Rouge, but…"

"But what?" Ambassador Rodney asked.

"When Earl Andrews got into the picture, everything went haywire."

"What do you mean?"

Rodney wanted to understand.

"He knew the twins were dealing with a great deal of money, so he had devised a plan to get a portion of the investments."

"Well, how did he do that?" Rodney asked.

"Earl Andrews has many business acquaintances from around the globe. The Angel Doll embezzlement has caused a lot of controversy in the underground. The earl's business partners had been secretly uncovering the details of the scandal. The earl of Scotland knew he could use the men from Barbados and get in on the dividends."

"Well, how did he maneuver the whole triangle of events to coincide with the murder of his wife"? the Ambassador from Argentina questioned.

"The earl of Scotland found out that the men were hired to murder Constance Stallings," Palmer responded. "And they would be paid an astronomical amount of money for the act. The studio had already called in on the novel and were making plans with the movie production company to make a movie. The director had been chosen, and the stars were being selected."

The ambassador of Argentina finally understood and said, "So, I can see now that Constance Stallings had to be murdered in order to secure the rights to the movie."

"Yes, and the earl of Scotland devised a plan to have his wife killed as a cover-up. Blaming the Barbados twins would ensure his inheritance would be safe, and he could claim the rights to the movie for himself. The Barbados twins were the key players, and if the earl eliminated them, he would be in the driver's seat."

The ambassador of Argentina was quite surprised and shocked to hear the news. "I cannot believe this has been going on right here under your leadership. I thought you had covered up all the details and nothing could go wrong."

"Well," Ambassador Leon Palmer said. "It probably would have worked beautifully. That is, until the earl decided that he wanted to be a part of the action so he would get a large portion of the money. The earl definitely wanted to be in on the two million that was sent to Zurich, Switzerland."

"So, what happened to the money from Baton Rouge?" Ambassador Rodney was puzzled.

"Private investigators for the D'La Chaisson trust finally confiscated the stolen money and got the money back to the states," Leon answered. "However," he said. "Several millions were not found. But the investigators were not concerned about the disappearance of money. Regardless, the Barbados twins are being held accountable for all the lost transactions, considering all the transactions took place on their private computer. The murder of Countess Christina Langley Andrews has been under speculation. The earl of Scotland says he has the proof that the Barbados twins killed his wife. If the truth was known, the earl probably had his wife killed and the time happened to coincide with the incident at Bellingfast Estates. And since he had a good alibi, he just pinned the murder on the twins."

Ambassador Rodney agreed. "I think you are right. Knowing the truth is one thing, and proving it is quite another thing."

"Regardless," said Palmer. "Do not let the twins return to the United Kingdom while we try analyze and figure this whole thing out."

"Got you," Rodney reassured him. "My surveillance is quite good, and I do not think they'll be doing very much while here in Buenos Aires."

"Good." The men were satisfied in their agreement and hung up the phone.

Back at Bellingfast Estate, the group from Louisiana was sitting in Lady Lindsey's room discussing the last incident.

"I cannot believe this is happening," Elizabeth Ann remarked. "I am ready to go home. I do not like this place anymore. It's inconceivable that all trips home have been denied."

Lady Lindsey then spoke to Reuben. "What is the latest information you've received from Charles Wolf regarding the Cayman Island and Singapore accounts?"

"Albert Buckley did a tremendous job locating all the funds and transactions that were confiscated from the Zurich account in Switzerland," Reuben announced. "The men from Barbados had tremendous skill in transferring the funds and transactions out of our bank accounts to their own overseas bank accounts. However, when the Hollywood scandal entered the picture, the sum of money and collateral exploded into the arena. How the earl of Scotland found out about this illegal transaction is still unknown. His plot to kill his wife left the Barbados men vulnerable. The earl has masterminded the rest of the scandal and extortion plot."

"Oh, I see," Lady Lindsey said. "That is why the earl could cash in on all of the money from the three accounts, including the money in the Zurich account. So, where does that leave us?"

Reuben continued, "Charles Wolfe counter-attacked and got our investments out with a loophole. That is, all our money is safe and in the banks in Baton Rouge and Lafayette."

"But, but, but..." Constance cried. "Where does that leave me? Somebody wants me dead."

"You will be safe while we are all here," Reuben said. "There are security guards and Scotland Yard police on the premises. They will be stationed here until this murder is solved."

"Now, can we return to the states?" Virginia Camille continued.

"Will I be safe when I get back home?" Constance cried.

"Well, yes," Reuben explained, "I would imagine you'll be safe back in the states. Whoever killed the countess was supposed to have killed you."

Constance raised her head in despair.

"It's getting late," Lady Lindsey noted. "Why don't we all retire for bed?"

"That's a good idea," said Reuben.

The rest of the group chimed in with approval. They all left Lady Lindsey's room, hopefully to get a good night's sleep.

Chapter 13

The Earl of Scotland Makes His Appearance

Early the next morning, the earl of Scotland, his bodyguards, and his own private detectives arrived at Bellingfast Estates in Northern Ireland. The Scotland Yard police had notified Madam MaRooska the night before to warn her of the visitors who would be arriving. When their vehicle began driving down the winding driveway, the Scotland Yard police had also been notified about the arrival, and the police had been instructed to let the men pass onto the premises.

When the car stopped at the entrance, Sir Callahan and Sir Richardson met the visitors.

Opening the door, Sir Callahan addressed the men, saying, "Madam MaRooska has been expecting you all morning. I'll take you all into her office."

Sir Callahan led the party of four into Madam MaRooska's chambers. As he knocked on the door, he stated, "Madam MaRooska, the men have arrived."

"Show them in, Sir Callahan," Madam MaRooska responded. "Please show them in."

Once inside her office chambers, the men all sat down.

The earl of Scotland spoke first. "As you well know, I am here on behalf of my deceased wife, Countess Langley Andrews. I understand Scotland Yard has done a thorough investigation concerning the murder. However, I have decided to do my own investigation."

"Scotland Yard has been handling all of the matters concerning civil, state, and judicial matters for well over fifteen years," Madam MaRooska said quite sternly. "We trust them completely. I see no need to have your interference. Unless, of course, you have a court order on us."

"We might just have to do that," the earl responded.

"So be it," Madam MaRooska urged. "I suggest that you return to Scotland Yard and talk with their detectives. Then, if need be, you can collaborate with these policemen, and you all can work together on this matter. However, under no circumstances will I allow you or your detectives to take over this investigation. Now, gentlemen, I feel it is best for you all to leave. No more questions. And you may use Scotland Yard as your legal source."

Back at Scotland Yard, one of the policemen on duty stated, "We received a call from Edmund Spencer. He was inquiring about the countess's unexplainable and unexpected death."

"Who is he?" Commissioner Sir Basil Thomson inquired.

The police officer reported what Edmund Spencer had told him. "He said that he was a friend of Countess Christina, and that she had been staying at his summer residence for the past six months."

"Why did he call?" Deputy Commissioner Stewart Menzies questioned.

The policeman on duty continued to explain. "He was genuinely concerned about the murder. He knew the earl of Scotland. The countess told Edmund that her husband had been exploiting her trust funds for several years for his own endeavors. The countess had her own private investigators follow him for the past two years. She was almost ready to take him to court."

"So, I ask again," Commissioner Thomson said, clarifying his question, "Why did he call us?"

"He wanted us to be very familiar with what had been going on prior to the murder," the police officer said. "Edmund knew the countess's husband could be a prime suspect."

"A very possible suspect," Sir Stewart Menzies emphasized.

Later that afternoon, a phone call came into Scotland Yard.

"Scotland Yard headquarters, Commissioner Sir Basil Thomson speaking. Who? What? Well, come on down to the station right now."

Assistant Commissioner Menzies walked back into the room. "Who was that?" he asked.

"Strange as it may seem," the commissioner replied. "It was the earl of Scotland. He and his own private investigators are on their way to see us, apparently with some valuable information concerning the death of the countess."

"Well, how interesting," said Menzies. "Considering the phone call I received from Sir Edmund last week. It should be an interesting meeting."

About an hour had gone by when the earl of Scotland and his two private investigators arrived.

As the earl walked in, he introduced himself, saying, "I am the earl of Scotland and husband of the late Countess Christina Langley Andrews. We have been at the Bellingfast Estates. We tried to talk to Madam MaRooska, but she had no intention of talking with us."

"I'm sure you gentlemen realize that we are the legal authorities and judicial counsel concerning all the matters within our jurisdiction," Sir Basil Thomson explained.

"Yes," the earl agreed. "Madam MaRooska made that clear. However, I do not feel we need your help anymore. My private investigators are going to handle this matter from here on out. We have absolute proof that the twins from Barbados planned and initiated the whole murder."

"Well, please sit down and explain in detail what you think happened," Menzies requested.

"First of all," Stewart Menzies said. "Why would these men want to murder your wife?"

The earl of Scotland quickly answered, "Money, money, money. You realize the countess was a very wealthy woman. She was a woman of prestige, culture, and above all she was in complete control of all of Scotland. Her father was a direct descendent of James VI, the king of Scotland. She has inherited the family fortunes in stocks and bonds and the family trust."

"What was the motive?" Sir Basil Thomson asked.

"With the Countess dead, her nephew, William Henry, inherits her part of the estate," The earl explained. "I have proof that the Barbados twins were hired by William Henry Stewart."

"Show us proof! Show us proof!" Menzies demanded.

When the investigator opened his briefcase, there was a notarized legal document detailing that William Henry Stewart would pay the twins upfront a substantial amount of money.

Menzies abruptly spoke up. "How did you come across this information?"

"Well, it is common knowledge that everybody knew the circumstances. William Henry is the next in line for the family fortune. I am very protective and concerned about the welfare of my wife's estate. I felt it was my responsibility to ensure that she received all the wealth and inheritance to which she was entitled."

The deputy commissioner then asked, "Who is supposed to receive the inheritance now?"

"Why, me," the Earl answered. "After all, I am her spouse."

"Oh, I see," Sir Basil Thomson said. "I see. Yes, I see."

The earl nodded. "Yes, now you see, I just wanted the countess to receive what was rightfully hers, and, of course, I want the killers to receive what they deserve."

Menzies parroted the earl's words. "Certainly you are only concerned with your wife's safety."

"And the large inheritance," Sir Basil Thomson added.

At these comments, the Earl seemed a bit perplexed. "What does that mean?"

"Well, you could possibly be the one that murdered the countess," the commissioner responded. "You do have a motive, don't you?"

"Nonsense, I do not need the countess's money. I am a wealthy man myself," bragged the Earl.

Sir Basil Thomson questioned, "Are you? If you are so wealthy, you would not need to confiscate her accounts to be included in your dividends."

"I will sue all of you for slander!" the Earl yelled at the commissioners. "I have never tampered with her money. I am appalled that you would say such a thing."

"I would suggest that you go back to Scotland," the deputy commissioner responded. "And be sure all your stories add up. We can secure all the bank statements if your alibi is correct, and it can be proven. Then you will be off the list of possible suspects."

"Let's go," the earl told his inspectors. "And you, Mr. Commissioner, you will be hearing from me again."

The three men left the police headquarters.

"We have got a lot of work to do," the commissioner announced.

"Yes," Menzies replied. "If Edmund Spencer has accurate information, then we have a pretty good lead."

The two men knew they had to search all the files for any new information.

"Why don't you and Inspector William Norwood check all the banks in Scotland to see where the countess had her bank accounts?" Sir Basil advised. "And get started immediately."

"Then we can contact those leads," Menzies said. "And we should be able to get some current updates on withdrawals and additional funds that have been added to the earl's private accounts."

"Be sure and keep an accurate account of the dates that the money was drained," Sir Basil Thomson ordered.

"Mr. Spencer said that the countess knew her husband had been transferring the money for several years."

"This should be easy to track," Menzies assured the commissioner. "We'll get started on this right away. I'll drive into Scotland this afternoon."

Both commissioners looked puzzled and pondered how the angel doll fit into this whole scheme of events.

"I really do not know," Sir Basil Thomson said. "I really do not know."

Chapter 14

The Guests Finally Depart for Home

Back at Bellingfast Estates, all was seemingly calm. The investigation had let up. Madam MaRooska had gotten a call from Scotland Yard. It looked like the mysterious murder was about to be solved. New information had been obtained, and the offices at Scotland Yard had intel from reliable sources that a possible suspect had been identified. Scotland Yard notified Madam MaRooska that her guests were now free to leave the resort.

"Great, great news!" Madam MaRooska declared. "My guests can now leave Bellingfast. This has been quite an ordeal for them. These incidents caused quite an uproar."

The announcement was made to all guests. All of them were ready to leave. But it was obvious that Scotland Yard was not disclosing who the murderer was or why the countess had been murdered. It was apparent that none of the guests at Bellingfast Estates for the past three weeks were possible suspects. The week delay was somewhat disturbing to all of them. Overall, each guest had had a wonderful time.

Back in the kitchen at Bellingfast Estates, the staff was discussing the departure of the guests.

"Well, we had another exciting event. I do believe most of the guests really enjoyed themselves," Gertrude remarked.

"Of course, the death of the countess took top priority," Sissily added.

"Yes," Sir Callahan remarked. "Another unsolved death. We all thought the Barbados twins were responsible, but Scotland Yard called, telling us another suspect is under investigation. The Barbados twins must have been eliminated."

"So, where did they get off to?" Gertrude asked.

"The limousine driver said that he dropped the men off at a small airport," Sir Callahan said, clarifying, "The Belfast City Airport. A huge jet was waiting for the men, and the limousine driver saw the jet take off."

"But where did they go?" Sissily questioned.

"Who knows?" Sir Richardson asked. "The commissioner at Scotland Yard did not seem interested in trying to locate them. I would presume they are not under investigation. Police headquarters had them for two days. And during the investigation, they were suspected of transferring some illegal documents to a Swiss bank account. However, the commissioner could not directly tie them to the murder of the countess."

Sir Callahan smiled. "I know Madam MaRooska is quite pleased with their findings. She does not like the bad publicity for the resort."

"However, sometimes Scotland Yard does not really know what goes on here," Mrs. Hatfield said. "Or they refuse to acknowledge that the activities at Madam MaRooska's Specialty Resort has anything to do with the troublesome mishaps at Bellingfast Estates."

"We will all agree to that fact," Gertrude declared.

"Sir Hightower was impressed with Lady Constance Stallings," Sir Callahan observed.

"I heard him chatting with her earlier," Sir Richardson noted. "He was making plans to go to the states to see her again."

"How did Charles Wellington fair?" Gertrude inquired.

"I think he always enjoys meeting new acquaintances, but as far as making any long-lasting relationships, he'll probably end up here next year. He will be hoping to find that special someone."

Madam MaRooska stuck her head in the door and said, "The guests are beginning to arrive in the dining hall. Are you ready to serve the departure and farewell dinner?"

"Yes, ma'am," Gertrude answered. "The serving trays are lined up near the butler's pantry. Sissily is stationed in position where she will place the trays on the dumb waiter as they travel up to the main floor."

As the guests came into the room, Reuben and Elizabeth Ann were in the front of the line. They found their seats at the lower end of the table near the ballroom. Doctor Harriet Asbury, Edward Harper, and Sir Hightower all came in together and looked around for their place cards. They found their seats and sat down. When Constance made her way to the table, she was incredibly happy to be seated next to Sir Hightower. Lady Lindsey and Virginia Camille walked in together. Doctor Wellington spied Virginia Camille across the room. He immediately approached her and escorted her to the seat next to him. Madam MaRooska had already made her way to the head of the table, and the rest of the guests meandered in and looked for their seats.

After a few minutes, all the places were finally full, except for those arranged for the Barbados twins. The brothers never arrived, and their seats were vacant. Madam MaRooska was somewhat frustrated. She knew the dinner was ready to be served, and she was disgusted that the men from Barbados were not present. Madam MaRooska kept looking at the grand clock in the dining hall. When the clock struck five, she knew she was not going to wait any longer.

Madam MaRooska stood to greet her guests for the final farewell.

"I'm meeting with you all again for our final farewell. It has been a wonderful affair. The time has flown by. I hope you made new and interesting acquaintances and friends. Madam MaRooska's Specialty Resort events are known worldwide. I just want to thank you all again for participating with us here at Bellingfast Estates for the spring event. We look forward each year to meeting interesting and intriguing people from around the globe. We have had famous doctors, famous literary persons, and famous and well-known anthropologists and sociologists with us here at our resort. You will never experience anything like this in any part of the world. You have shared something special with these extraordinary guests here at our resort. Please, when you return home, take these experiences from our famous guests and share them with your friends and family.

"I feel that I must make mention of this fact: I work closely with Scotland Yard when any type of accident occurs here at this resort. Sir Basil Thomson and Stewart Menzies have assured me that there is definite proof that none of our guests were involved with the horrendous murder of Countess Christina Langley Andrews of Scotland. Scotland Yard never divulged the suspect or suspects under investigation, but they assure me that they will issue an indictment soon. Please, if you would like to make reservations for the next fall or spring event, do so.

"Our staff wishes you a farewell and a safe trip home. Please enjoy your lunch, and after lunch, you are free to leave. Again, thank you for your patience during this time after the tragic death of Countess Christina. The limousines are out front, and the staff here at Bellingfast will take care of your luggage needs as you depart. Bon voyage, and thank you again for choosing to attend our spectacular event."

The guests stood and applauded in appreciation for the exciting visit. After the lunch, the guests began to depart for the airport. The limousines left Bellingfast Estates.

The five guests from Louisiana were riding together and discussing all they had experienced in the past two weeks.

"With all the turmoil and excitement—" Lady Lindsey began.

"And worry," Virginia Camille interjected.

"Did you finish your novel?" Lady Lindsey finished.

"Surprisingly yes," Lady Constance answered. "And I do believe this novel will be a bestseller. The suspense and thrill of the unsolved murder at Bellingfast just added to the conclusion of the book. When a novel has unexplained events and strange circumstances, one must conclude that a story of this nature will be read and enjoyed for decades for those trying to figure out the truth as it was intimately told."

"I'm only glad we solved all of the financial problems," Reuben concluded. "When I received the call from Mother's financial advisor, I was dumbfounded, wondering how this could have happened under our noses. Now, I know this conspiracy had been going on for more than a year. The legal document drafts and transactions had been going on for well over a year. The cover up was organized, and the conspiracy was undetectable. When Charles began to investigate, the situation was already apparent. The illegal transactions had already taken place."

"I'm only glad your mother did not have to get involved in the scandal," Lady Lindsey said. "I do not know if her health could have taken all the turmoil and stress."

"She was in no condition to face this catastrophic event," Reuben stated.

As the guests were riding, they could see airport was nearby.

"I'm only glad that we are all safe," Virginia Camille remarked. "This has been an interesting and intriguing three weeks."

"Very memorable, I have to say," Constance agreed.

"Now we are finally on our way home," Lady Lindsey interjected. "Overall, it was a very pleasurable trip."

"I am glad that we are are on our way home," Constance said, and then admitted, "But this trip allowed us to meet some remarkably interesting people from all over the world, and I did finish my novel, *The Angel Doll*."

About the Author

Margaret Joanne Rice is a retired educator. She holds a Master's Degree from Mississippi State University. She has taught elementary school and served as a guidance counselor at the Middle and High School levels. The author has always had a desire to write and has dabbled with the desire for years. It was hard to write before retirement because of obligations to family and work. Those years raising three children hindered the writing process. Ten years ago, the writer was forced to retire because of a kidney transplant. The children were grown, and suddenly, she had time to write.

Also Available from this Author

ISBN: 978-1-944486-48-8
Visit www.amazon.com
Author: Margaret Joanne Rice

Set in the Old South after the Civil War– specifically on a tobacco plantation in Staunton, Virginia– this story revolves around three key groups of people. Plantation owners, plantation workers, and Native Americans play integral roles in this saga. They often intersect and prove necessary for each other to exist in their sociopolitical climate. The conflict in the story involves an ancient Indian folktale about a baby skull hidden on plantation property in a grandfather clock that is shrouded in superstition. This skull is said to have magical powers, and when it disappears, many strange events begin to unfold.

Also Available from this Author

Also Available from J. Kenkade Publishing

ISBN: 978-1-944486-55-0
Visit www.amazon.com
Author: Garrett Cottrell

In this dystopian novel, a group of teens with superhuman strength find out through a group of Hunters that they must either go on the run to survive or be forced to go to camps set aside for "Abnormals." They decide to go on the run and train in their newly found powers. They gain friends and lose friends along the way, but they fight well together.

Also Available from J. Kenkade Publishing

ISBN: 978-1-944486-88-7
Visit www.amazon.com
Author: Marshall B Crowder and Luz Eneida Torres

The Wanderer's Enduring Love is a love story that spans centuries. Beginning in the 18th century with Lusamba and Marcelo. A young couple full of life and love that get torn apart by the brutal transatlantic slave trade. In a second attempt at love, Lusamba tries again with Elias, only to be horrifically denied. Modern day couple Neida and Marcel meet on a dating site and immediately realize that they have too much in common for their meeting to be merely coincidental. They decide to explore any connections they might have through DNA testing and soon discover that they have a shared past. Are they prepared for what they might discover? How are they connected? Will what they find bring them closer or tear them apart? Follow them and travel to Cameroon, Puerto Rico, California, Georgia, and Arkansas. See how they use modern technology to uncover the past and discover their future.

Also Available from J. Kenkade Publishing

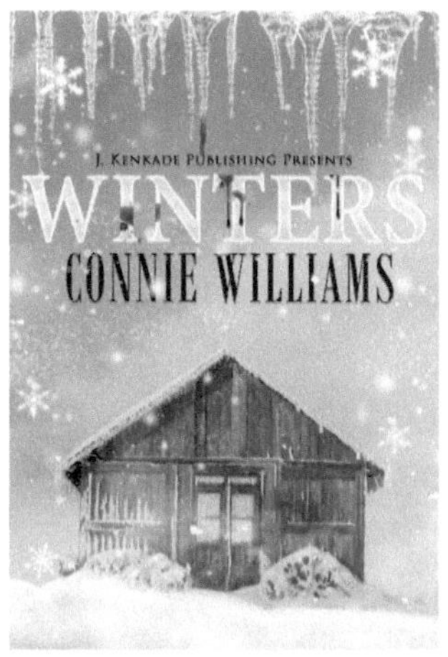

ISBN: 978-1-944486-40-2
Visit www.amazon.com
Author: Connie Williams

Winters is a captivating and passionate Christian suspense novel about a powerful, spiritual black family who is anointed and ordained by God Almighty. You will feel love, pain, heartaches, compassion, grace, mercy, suffering, and God's spirit, all in one story. Find out why Winters is about the coldest season of the year in more ways than one. Come and live in the minds and hearts of Stella, Abe, Mr. Perkins, The Langley family, Hattie, Benjamin, and Minnie. So much more awaits you in this powerful Christian suspense novel. Both fiction and nonfiction, Winters will give you a chill like never before!

www.ingramcontent.com/pod-product-compliance
Lightning Source LLC
Chambersburg PA
CBHW020444270626
47155CB00022B/1510

* 9 7 8 1 9 4 4 4 8 6 8 7 7 *